AF557791

Books by Meena Arora Nayak

The Rabbit in the Moon: Two Tales from the Panchatantra

The Four Avengers versus the Elephant: Two Tales from the Panchatantra

How the Greedy Crane Was Killed by the Clever Crab: Two Stories from the Panchatantra

The Monkey's Revenge: Two Stories from the Panchatantra

The Girl in the Magical Flute: Stories from Myths and Folktales of India

The Panchatantra of Vishnusharma: A Retelling

Adbhut: Marvellous Creatures of Indian Myth and Folklore

The Kathasaritsagara of Somadeva: A Retelling

The Blue Lotus: Myths and Folktales of India

A Dust Storm in Delhi

Evil in Mahabharata

Endless Rain

About Daddy

In the Aftermath

The Puffin Book of Legendary Lives

The Undead Ghoul and the Clever Raja

The Undead Ghoul and the Clever Raja

Twenty-five Tales
of the *Vetala Panchavimshati*

A RETELLING BY
MEENA ARORA NAYAK

ALEPH

ALEPH BOOK COMPANY
An independent publishing firm
promoted by ***Rupa Publications India***

First published in India in 2025
by Aleph Book Company
161-B/4, Gulmohar House,
Yusuf Sarai Community Centre,
New Delhi 110049

This is a work of fiction. Names, characters, places, and incidents are either the product of the author's imagination or are used fictitiously and any resemblance to any actual persons, living or dead, events, or locales is entirely coincidental.

ISBN: 978-93-6523-888-4

1 3 5 7 9 10 8 6 4 2

Printed in India

Didi, Veerji, Kiran, and Sudha, this is for you and for the memories of our Chandamama *days.*

Contents

I bow to Maheshwara
who makes the immovable mountains whirl
as he moves his arms with the rhythm
of the wonderous and fearsome Tandava.
Shesha's thousand raised hoods quiver
underneath the dancing feet of the Lord
whose wild jatta, tawny as bumblebees,
swirl and swing in majestic waves
while a crescent moon shines atop.

I bow to Hari
whose mind is fixed on the three worlds
whose auspicious feet are the source
of all happiness and by whose grace
one gains knowledge and good fortune.

These twenty-five tales—
divine and full of curious flavours—
may they be preserved in memory.

Good people,
if you would like to know these tales
read them here in written form.

Author's Note

The present work is my attempt to retell the classic tales of the *Vetala Panchavimshati* in a form, style, and language that would appeal to the modern reader. I have also attempted to capture in these stories the piquant humour and the subtle wisdom that characterize this ancient text.

To bring together the best of its different versions, I have used several different iterations: *Vetala Panchavimshati* of both Shivadasa and Jambhaladatta, the vetala story cycle included in Somadeva's *Kathasaritsagara*, *Baital Pachisi* of Lallu Ji Lal's, and other adaptations of Vikram–Vetala story collections. The number, arrangement, and narrative of the tales follow Shivadasa's rendition, which most scholars consider to be the closest to the Urtext. However, readers who are familiar with this text will also see the following variances:

VIKRAMADITYA'S CITY

Shivadasa and Somadeva make Pratishthana Vikramaditya's ruling city; however, I have chosen to place him in Ujjayini. This is how he is often portrayed in folklore. Even his buried lion throne that Raja Bhoja discovers, as described in *Simhasana Dvatrimshika,* is in Ujjayini. In addition, *Vetala Panchavimshati* is set in a cremation ground that is near Shipra River, which flows through Ujjayini (modern-day Ujjain). Pratishthana, on the other hand, as we learn from various literatures, was not only ruled by Vikramaditya's enemy, Shalivahana, but it may also have been where Vikramaditya was fatally wounded in battle.

RELIGIOUS ORIENTATION OF THE TANTRIC YOGI

I have chosen to follow Jambhaladatta's version in describing the yogi as a Shaiva-Shakta kapalika, as opposed to Shivadasa's version, in which he is a Digambara monk, quite likely a Jain. Here are my reasons: although in medieval India, tantra vidya was prevalent in all four traditions—Buddhist, Jain, Shaiva, and Shakta—the rituals described in the text align most closely with the practices of the latter two. Additionally, parts of the frame story that relate to the yogi in the *Vetala Panchavimshati* reflect the origin myth of the Kapalika sect, which is Shaiva. For instance, according to this myth, Kalabhairava has to wander the earth for twelve years with Brahma's head (kapala) stuck to his palm to expiate his sin of brahmanicide. Similarly, the yogi in the *Vetala Panchavimshati* does twelve years of sadhana to achieve his goal and every day of those years he woos Vikramaditya to secure his assistance. (This origin myth of the Kapalika sect is included in the 'Introduction' of this adaptation.)

PROLOGUE

While most of the story related in the prologue of this present retelling closely follows Shivadasa's text, I have altered it a little to include portions from Lallu Ji Lal's Hindi translation. For instance, the latter has a preceding story that is not in the Shivadasa version. In addition, Shivadasa's extant text is missing the beginning sentences. Hence, I have improvised by using the beginning from Lallu Ji Lal's *Baital Pachisi*.

THE CORPSE

In Shivadasa's *Vetala Panchavimshati*, the corpse is described as blue and skeletal. While this is definitely a more macabre image, I have made the corpse fresh and full-bodied. A key reason for this is Lallu Ji Lal's description of the first interaction between Vikramaditya and the vetala, which is different from Shivadasa's. In Lal's text, when Vikramaditya cuts the dead body loose, it cries out as it hits the ground, making Vikramditya think that the man may still be alive. I have incorporated this scene, because I feel that the mischievousness of the vetala aptly sets the stage for the convoluted tales he is about to narrate. In terms of the corpse—for Vikramaditya to be fooled into believing that the man is alive, the corpse needs to be whole and undecayed, not a skeleton. Aside from this narrative verisimilitude, in the practice of vetala sadhana, too, the corpse must be fresh and unspoiled. Additionally, the story specifically states that the corpse hangs from a shisham tree. This tree is a symbol of non-decay; hence it can be assumed that the corpse has not decomposed. (See explanation in the 'Introduction'.)

FORM AND STYLE

Shivadasa's *Vetala Panchavimshati* is in champu-kavya, a genre that was popular in literary compositions of ancient and medieval India. Champu is a stylized combination of prose and verse, with the events of the narrative described in prose and authorial didacticism stated in verse. I have decided to use only prose, as it is in Jambhaladatta's text. However, deviating from his bare-boned narratives and repetitive epithets and similes, I have also included some of Shivadasa's stylization. There are several reasons why I have not used verse. Firstly, the setting of the stories is a cremation ground and the narrator is a vetala; therefore, this can be seen as a sort of ghost story. Stories in this genre are most effective when they are short and crisp and carry a punch. Verse, especially didactic, weighs the narrative down. Secondly, the plots of these stories have many twists and turns and unexpected endings; thus, to break the narrative action with several stanzas of verse, as Shivadasa does, is to lose not just the tightness of the plot but also the surprise element of the climax. Thirdly, each story has a time constraint. It must conclude before Vikramaditya reaches the yogi so that the vetala can whisk the corpse back to the shisham tree. Additionally, the vetala must tell twenty-four tales before the end of the night to allow the tantric yogi enough time to perform the rituals before sunrise. Therefore, extending the stories with multiple verses and aphorisms, while in keeping with the norm of wisdom literature, is contrary to the tight schedule that the vetala has to keep. Finally, there is the motivation of the vetala's character. He is a trickster and it would be uncharacteristic of him to spout wisdom; instead, one would expect him to deliberately keep his narrations cryptic to confound Vikramaditya and the reader. The vetala's riddle question at the end of each story, combined with Vikramaditya's answer, amply demonstrates this purpose. Taking all these elements into account, I have decided to tell the stories entirely in prose. However, within the narrative of the stories, I have incorporated a few relevant nuggets from Shivadasa's epigrammatic verses that emphasize the text's comment on societal norms and human behaviour.

TITLING THE STORIES

All versions of *Vetala Panchavimshati* that I know of base each story's title on the name of its main character. This is a common practice in Indian folklore and there are many wonderful reasons for this: the meaning of the character's name reveals the intent of the story; the name establishes the character as a hero and facilitates the story's popularity, especially as an oral tale; these characters and their names become part of the idiom, creating behavioural paradigms. The best example of this is Sheikh Chilli, the weed-smoking daydreamer, whose name has forever become synonymous with all daydreamers. I have chosen to title the stories differently. My main reason is that in translation it is difficult to employ a name to characterize a story without first explaining the meaning of the name and, in doing so, the fluidity and cleverness of the wordplay (in the name) are lost. Another reason is my perception that the title of a story is like a window but curtained to retain its mystery. For me, the riddle question that the vetala asks Vikramaditya at the end of each tale is its window, because it pinpoints the key narrative question and moulds the reader's interpretation of the story; yet it is cryptic enough to not give away any spoilers. Therefore, each story's title in the present work is based on the question that the vetala asks Vikramaditya.

BENEDICTION

Shivadasa's and Somadeva's texts begin with praise to Ganesha, asking for his continued indulgence and parental love. Jambhaladatta's benediction, on the other hand, consists of several verses, the first two of which refer to Shiva and his Tandava, his dance of annihilation. I feel that the latter's reference to Shiva and the Tandava is most fitting for a book whose frame story is based in Shaiva tantra, whose narrator possesses dead bodies, and whose setting is a cremation ground. Therefore, the invocation in this present retelling is a selection from Jambhaladatta's benedictory verses.

Introduction

The story of *Vetala Panchavimshati* begins with a king receiving a small fruit as a gift from a tantric yogi every day for twelve years. The king hands the fruit to his minister whose job is to take all official gifts, big and small, and put them in the treasury. This item is so tiny and insignificant that the minister does not even bother to open the treasury door to deposit it. He just drops it into the room through the lattice of a window. Then, one day, as the yogi presents the fruit and the king attempts to pass it to his minister, it slips out of his hand and drops to the floor. The king's pet monkey, who is sitting on the royal shoulder, leaps and grabs the fruit. When he puts it between his teeth and cracks it open, out pops a gem so precious and dazzling that everyone in the courtroom is astounded. The king, too, is amazed, but then realization dawns on him and, turning to his minister of gifts, he asks, urgently, 'What have you done with all the fruits that the yogi has been giving me?' Fearing for his job, the minister rushes to the treasury room to check. There, under the window, he finds a mound of smelly, rotting fruits and amidst them, thousands of glittering jewels.

The following day, when the yogi returns to give the king another fruit, the king stops him. 'First tell me why you've been giving me these precious gems for all these years?' he asks. The yogi requests to speak to the king in private and tells him that he is in the process of gaining siddhis (supernatural powers). 'I need a man of valour and determination to help me achieve this goal,' he says to the king. 'How can I help?' the king asks, and the yogi replies, 'There's a dead body hanging from a shisham tree in the cremation ground. I want you to bring me that body.'

On the assigned day, the king goes to the cremation ground, finds the corpse hanging in the shisham tree, and cuts it loose. However, when the body hits the ground, it cries out in pain. The king thinks that the person is still alive, but he soon realizes that the body is possessed by a vetala, who is playing tricks on him. Undeterred by this, the king hefts the corpse on his shoulder and starts walking towards the bargad tree, under which the tantric yogi is waiting for him. The vetala in the body then speaks to him and, just for the fun of it, tells him a story. At the end of it, he asks the king a riddling question related to it with a warning that if he knows the answer and does not give it, his head will explode into a thousand pieces. The king gives an answer; however, as soon as he speaks it, the corpse flies off his shoulder and hangs itself back in the shisham tree. Returning to the tree, the king cuts the corpse loose and throws it over his shoulder again, but when he starts to walk towards the bargad, the vetala tells him another story, which also ends with a question. The king answers this question as well, but, as soon as he does, the corpse is back in the tree. In this way, the vetala tells the king twenty-four tales and the king makes twenty-four attempts to bring the corpse to the tantric yogi so that he can use it for shava-sadhana (knowledge of raising a corpse) to acquire magical powers.

WHO IS VIKRAMADITYA?

This brave, valorous, resolute king, who is engaged in the Sisyphean task of bringing the corpse to the tantric yogi, is Raja Vikramaditya of Malwa, the legendary hero of many ancient tales. In fact, his legend is so large that he is counted among India's greatest kings, such as Ashoka and Akbar,[1] even though, unlike these historical figures, Vikramaditya's historicity is dubious. It is possible that there was a real Raja Vikramaditya at the turn of the era, who was the king of Malwa and whose kingship was such that he was extolled by travelling bards and storytellers. Or, perhaps, he was wholly fictitious—a hero whose persona and celebrity were simply a flight of fancy, created by these storytellers to entertain the audiences. More than likely, Vikramaditya was both, a product of imaginative minds and a reigning monarch, possibly of Malwa; although, proof of his existence is scant and incidental. One connection that is often made to validate him is the Hindu calendar, Vikrami Samvat, which is attributed to him. According to some accounts, this Samvat was created in 58 BCE. However, 'since a ruler by this name important enough to start an era is not known in the first century', the link between Vikramaditya and the eponymous calendar is probably mythological or of a later date.[2] Moreover, this Samvat was initially not known as Vikram; it was called either Malwa or Krita. It became associated with Vikramaditya only in the eighth century CE.[3]

Most scholars believe that the Vikramaditya of stories and legends is the fourth–fifth-century-CE Gupta monarch, Chandra Gupta II, who took the title of Vikramaditya. A significant piece of evidence they cite to correlate Chandra Gupta II with the titular Vikramaditya is the historical

---

[1]*Simhāsana Dvātriṃśikā Thirty-Two Tales of the Throne of Vikramaditya*, A. N. D. Haksar (trans.), London: Penguin Books, 1998, p. x.

[2]Romila Thapar, *The Penguin History of Early India: From the Origins to AD 1300*. London, NY: Penguin Books, 2002, p. 220.

[3]D. C. Sircar, 'SPREAD OF THE MALAVA ERA', *Proceedings of the Indian History Congress*, Vol. 15, 1952, pp. 371–74.

record stating that the Malwa king, Vikramaditya, drove out the Shakas from Ujjain. The date of this great victory also corresponds with the ouster of the Shakas from the 'region of Kutch, Kathiawar and Malwa in Western India', where they ruled till the late fourth century CE.[4] Chandra Gupta II may or may not have been the 'Vikramaditya' of this incident, but, according to Vishakhadatta's play, *Devi-Chandraguptam*, that was written two centuries after the reign of Chandra Gupta II, he is, indeed, the very same monarch. This is how the incident is dramatized: Samudra Gupta's elder son, Rama Gupta, was defeated by the Shaka chief and had to forfeit his kingdom and wife, Dhruvadevi. However, when the queen was delivered to the Shakas, it was not Dhruvadevi but the younger prince, Chandra, dressed as her. He destroyed the Shakas, saved Dhruvadevi, and regained the kingdom. This victory brought him great fame and public adoration; so much so that his brother, Rama, became resentful and turned against him. Ultimately, Chandra Gupta killed Rama and married the queen, Dhruvadevi.[5]

Chandra Gupta II was a great monarch who is hailed not only for his military victories but also for his kingship. His reign 'marks the high watermark of ancient Indian culture' in which 'most [people were] prosperous and happy beneath his sceptre'.[6] Thus, the legend of Vikramaditya—Sun of Valour—fits Chandra Gupta II quite well.

The Gupta period was also when charitra literature (historical biographies) was on the rise. Sanskrit had become politicized, and scholars of Sanskrit had begun to appropriate

[4]Thapar, *Penguin History of Early India,* p. 223–24.

[5]Ibid., p. 285.

[6]A. L. Basham, *The Wonder that Was India,* Calcutta: Rupa & Co., 1954, p. 66.

the work of bards and sutas (storytellers of mixed race) by travelling across kingdoms and seeking employment as biographers on hire. Titles were also legitimized, 'along with [a monarch's] connection to ancient heroes and earlier rulers'.[7] The title of Vikramaditya was popular among kings, because not only was it a testament to a monarch's fearlessness and majesty, but it was also resonant of mythological solar dynasties. Thus, many kings assumed this title and each king's accomplishments were incorporated into the legend. This lends credence to the inference that Vikramaditya may not have been just one king but an appellative for an amalgamation of kings and kingly traits.

This consolidation of monarchical qualities is profiled in the thirty-two throne stories of *Simhasana Dvatrimsika*, which are commonly believed to celebrate Vikramaditya, the ruler, but they may very well also explicate Vikramaditya the title. Additionally, this may explain why different forms of Vikramaditya's name appear in different texts and contexts: Vikrama (valorous), Vikramasena (valorous in battle), Vishamsheela (harsh yet gentle), Trivikramaditya (victorious in the three worlds), Vikramakesari (the valorous lion), etc. In addition, the locale in which he is placed varies from story to story and, sometimes, even within the same story or story cycle. For instance, in Somadeva's *Kathasaritsagara*, which contains not only the vetala story cycle but also different versions of tales that are not part of this cycle, the protagonist of the vetala stories is the ruler of Pratishthana, a city on the bank of Godavari; in a different version of the frame story, he is the ruler of Malwa; and in another story cycle, he is the king of Ujjayini. In Shivadasa's rendition of *Vetala Panchavimshati*,

[7]Thapar, *Penguin History of Early India*, p. 394.

which is considered closest to the lost Urtext, he is also placed in Pratishthana.

Vikramaditya's connection to Pratishthana adds to the mystery that surrounds him. Pratishthana was ruled by the famous Shalivahana, who, according to various literary sources, was a sworn enemy of the ruler of Malwa. In fact, some of these accounts state that Vikramaditya was killed in a battle with Shalivahana. For instance, the sixth tale of the prologue of *Simhasana Dvatrimsika* describes how Vikramaditya learns, through premonition and omens, that Shalivahana is his destroyer, and, to pre-empt him, he mounts an attack on Pratishthana. However, Shalivahana is the fabled son of Shesha Naga and that celestial snake helps him defeat and kill Vikramaditya.

The legend of Vikramaditya owes much of its existence to literary works and even those in which he is not the key protagonist add to his fame. This sort of intertextuality of a legendary character's persona certainly furthers a literary tradition. But its prolificity also strengthens the probability that the character may have had roots in reality. To name a few of these works: in Ananda's *Madhavanala-Kamakandala-Katha,* Vikramaditya helps unite the lovers Madhavanala and Kamakandala; in *Vikramodya,* he is a wise-talking parrot; in the Jain text *Panchadandachhatra-Prabandha,* Vikramaditya is a powerful magician; and Ananta's *Viracharitra* describes the struggles of Vikramaditya and Shalivahana.[8]

The two most popular texts that elevate Vikramaditya to the height of acclaim are the *Simhasana Dvatrimsika*, also known as *Singhasan Battisi*, or 'thirty-two tales of the throne', and the

---

[8]Maurice Winternitz, *A History of Indian Literature*, Subhadra Jha (trans.), Vol. 3, 5th ed., Delhi: Motilal Banarsidass Publishers, 2018, pp. 376–77.

Vetala Panchavimshati, or *Baital Pachisi* (Twenty-five tales of Baital), as it is commonly known. Both these are standalone texts, composed centuries apart, but they complement each other. The first four tales of *Simhasana Dvatrimsika* are the Kathamukha, or prologue to the *Vetala Panchavimshati.* Also, the thirty-first tale of the throne stories provides the plot line of the Vetala story cycle. The key difference between the two texts is that in *Vetala Panchavimshati,* Vikramaditya is the recipient of stories to which he has no relation, except as a passive listener, and in the *Simhasana Dvatrimsika,* the stories are mostly about him. In these, we see a monarch 'who shines brighter than a million suns, is as handsome as Kamadeva, as majestic as Indra, as benevolent as Shiva, and as just as Dharmaraja' (from 'How the Story Begins' in this retelling). He is brilliant, brave to a fault, learned, noble, heroic, magnanimous, and loved by both people and devas, especially Indra, who considers him a close friend. To put it succinctly: Vikramaditya is the ideal king.

The prologue of *Simhasana Dvatrimsika* adds another layer to Vikramaditya's lore. It describes how the renowned Raja Bhoja Paramara of Malwa finds a buried lion throne that is studded with precious gems and resting on a base of thirty-two stone statuettes. When Bhoj attempts to sit on it, the statuettes come alive and tell him that he must first prove himself worthy of the throne by demonstrating the qualities of the great king, Vikramaditya, whose throne this is. Bhoja then requests the statuettes to tell him the qualities that Vikramaditya possessed, and, one by one, each statuette relates a story that encapsulates a virtue of the great Chakravarti Raja Vikramaditya.

Raja Bhoja, who is a historical figure and ruled Malwa from 1018 to 1055 CE, aspired to be like Vikramaditya. Clearly, he believed that Vikramaditya was more than a legend. That is why earlier scholars surmised that *Simhasana Dvatrimsika* was composed at the court of Raja Bhoja, who was quite a polymath himself.[9] However, based on its references in other contemporaneous literatures, later scholarship dates this compilation of throne stories to no earlier than the thirteenth century.[10] These scholars also suggest that the *Vetala Panchavimshati* was an earlier text and probably preceded *Simhasana Dvatrimasika* by a few centuries.

DATING THE TEXT

It is difficult to date the *Vetala Panchavimshati*. Not only is the Urtext lost, but the early recensions that may have produced the various extant versions are also lost. Therefore, it is hard to determine what was precedent and what may have been interpolated in the compositions that have come down to us. The only way to arrive at a possible date of the text's original composition is through its literary allusions and references to social and cultural practices.

Some scholars believe that because the vetala story cycle first appeared in Kashmir in the eleventh-century compositions, Kshemendra's *Brihatkathamanjari* and Somadeva's *Kathasaritsagara,* that may have been the debut of *Vetala Panchavimshati*. However, two factors confute this assumption: these twenty-five tales are tightly structured with the linking device of the vetala and are a standalone cycle. Also, they are not at all integral to the main frame story of either *Brihatkathamanjari* or *Kathasaritsagara*. In fact, in Somadeva's work, they are even further removed and emboxed

---

[9]Franklin Edgerton, 'A Hindu Book of Tales: The Vikramacarita', *The American Journal of Philology*, Vol. 33, No. 3, 1912, p. 251.

[10]*Simhāsana Dvātriṃśikā*, Haksar (trans.), p. xv.

in a secondary frame of stories. Therefore, more than likely, the vetala story cycle was already in circulation at that time, and both Somadeva and Kshemendra inserted it in their works, because of its popularity.

The clearest frame of reference is of Chandra Gupta II (375–415 CE), who, as stated above, assumed the title of Vikramaditya and may have been the Vikramaditya of these tales.

An inference can also be drawn from the place names mentioned in the stories, because using specific locations in a narrative was a bardic technique to engage audiences. Not only did it demonstrate the bard's travel experience, but it also gave the audiences a sense of connection to locales with which they were familiar. The vetala stories are all set in different cities, across the Gupta Empire. For instance, Ujjayini, which was Chandra Gupta II's second capital, is the setting for several of the stories. Pataliputra, a centre for art and culture, is another setting. Other cities in which the stories occur, such as Varanasi, Anga, Shravasti, Kanyakubja, Vardhamana, Tamralipti were all flourishing urban centres in the Gupta period, especially in the fourth–fifth centuries.

The context of tantra is, perhaps, the most significant determinant. Tantric practices were relatively unknown till Chandra Gupta II's reign. Archaeological evidence from his reign suggests that even Shaivism was a fairly new belief system at that time, and *Shaiva Siddhanta*, which is considered the foundation of tantric traditions, was still in its early stages.[11] The earliest known tantra text, *Brahmayamala Tantra,* or *Pichumata,* was composed in the seventh century CE and it is

---

[11]Peter Bisschop, 'Śaivism in the Gupta-Vākāṭaka Age', *Journal of the Royal Asiatic Society*, Third Series, Vol. 20, No. 4, October 2010, p. 483.

noteworthy that some of the rituals detailed in it are similar to those described in the frame story of the *Vetala Panchavimshati*. Therefore, it can be surmised that *Vetala Panchavimshati* may have been laid down sometime in the seventh–eight centuries, or later, but it references the Gupta period.

POPULARITY AND SPREAD

Many stories of the *Vetala Panchavimshati,* without the element of the vetala, were popular narratives in circulation, before and after they were laid down in the text. This is the nature of folklore; not only is it a roving transmission of narratives, but it can also adapt to any milieu or textual tradition. For instance: the sixteenth tale (in the present adaptation)—the story of Unmadani—about an intoxicating beauty, whom a king unknowingly rejects and then desires so passionately that he dies from the angst, is found in two prominent texts—Kalhana's *Rajatarangini*, which is a chronicle of kings, and Somadeva's *Kathasaritsagara*, which is a vast repository of stories. Centuries later, this tale even made its way to the Indian film industry and was adapted into the classic 1960s film, *Chaudhvin Ka Chand*. The ninth tale, the story of Madanasena, a woman whose marriage vows are valued more by her lover and a robber than by herself, made an early appearance in a Buddhist Tripitaka text of the third century CE. The medieval versions of this also travelled around the world to be included in story cycles of *Alf Laylah wa-Laylah* (*Arabian Nights*), Boccaccio's *Decameron,* and the 'Franklin's Tale' in Chaucer's *Canterbury Tales.*[12] Then,

[12]Adeesh Sathaye, 'The scribal life of folktales in medieval India', *South Asian History and Culture,* Vol. 8, No. 4, 2017, pp. 430–47.

there is the Buddhist story of Jimutavahana (tale fifteen), the Bodhisattva who sacrifices his life to save a naga prince from being devoured by Garuda. This story is in several texts, including the *Kathasaritsagara*, and it is also the subject of *Naganada*, a seventh-century drama attributed to Harsha.

ADAPTATIONS OF SHIVADASA AND JAMBHALADATTA

The entire vetala story cycle, too, has many versions. Aside from the collections in Kshemendra's and Somadeva's compositions, two of the most known retellings are by Shivadasa and Jambhaladatta. Nothing of significance is really known about these two composers. Shivadasa was probably a Kayastha from Gujarat and belonged to a family of scribes. He reconstructed a Sanskrit text from different manuscripts in about 1387, which is the earliest dated, extant, unitary manuscript of *Vetala Panchavimshati*. Jambhaladatta's text, which is also in Sanskrit, is believed to have been composed in the sixteenth century.[13] Jambhaladatta may have been a king's minister who learned ministerial affairs from a guru named Varadatta, who is mentioned in the benediction of his composition.[14]

The Shivadasa and Jambhaladatta versions are different enough to suggest that each may have had its own predecessor. While the tales in both versions are similar, there are other key differences: Jambhaladatta's text is almost entirely in prose, with

---

[13]Susan Nádasdi, 'IDENTICAL STORIES IN THE TWENTY-FIVE TALES OF THE VETĀLA AND IN THE OCEANOF STORY', *Acta Orientalia Academiae Scientiarum Hungaricae*, Vol. 21, No. 3, 1968, p. 363.

[14]M. B. Emeneau (trans.), *Jambhaladatta's Version of the Vetālapañcavinśati : A Critical Sanskrit Text in Transliteration*, New Haven: American Oriental Society, 1934, p. xvii.

just a few verses scattered here and there; Shivadasa's, on the other hand, is composed in the stylized literary genre of champu-kavya that fluidly combines prose and verse. The number of stories also varies. In Shivadasa's version, there are twenty-four tales and the frame story makes it twenty-five. In Jambhaladatta, the frame story is in addition to the twenty-five tales, which suggests that the extra story may have been a later adoption. But the biggest contrast between the two versions is how they begin and end. Shivadasa's text has a prologue that binds together the yogi, corpse, and king through the circumstance of birth. Thus, their natal astrological charts establish a shared fate and destiny, which the yogi brings to a head with a murder and the king vindicates by destroying the yogi. In Jambhaladatta's version, on the other hand, not only is the relationship among the corpse, yogi, and king kept from the reader till the very end, but also it is no more than a relationship of competitors, with the corpse and the yogi as deceitful contenders of vetala siddhi and the king as simply a means to bring about a conclusion. This difference in the causal relationship between the three main players determines their agency, making Shivadasa's version more complex than Jambhaladatta's.

Another noteworthy difference among the versions is the tantric yogi's religious orientation. While his tantric pursuits remain the same in all versions, in Shivadasa's narrative, he is a Jain Digambar and in Jambhaladatta's, he is a Shaiva kapalika (skull-bearer). (In the earlier, *Kathasaritsagara,* he is a Buddhist Bhikshu.) This doctrinal characterization of the tantric yogi serves to situate each version in its religiopolitical climate and the prevailing belief system of the time. Therefore, it also leaves open the question of who the yogi may have been in the Urtext.

OTHER VERSIONS AND THE MOST POPULAR

Aside from these four best known versions of *Vetala Panchavimshati* (by Shivadasa, Jambhaladatta, Kshemendra, and Somadeva), there are other variant texts in several vernacular languages, such as Tamil, Marathi, Bengali, Telugu, Gujarati, etc. Most of these were later translations, and they all derived from one seventeenth-century version in Brajbhasha, entitled *Baital Pachisi,* which was translated from the Sanskrit by Surat Kabishwar, a court poet of Raja Jaisingh Sawai of Jaipur. In 1805, a Hindi/Hindustani version, also based on Kabishwar's Brajbhasha translation, was created by Lallu Ji Lal, and this *Baital Pachisi* became the most popular; so much so that it was used as an examination text for Military Service in the East India Company, because it was considered by the Raj as exemplary of the common native language.[15] In addition to Lallu Ji Lal's Hindi *Baital Pachisi,* British officers in India used an Urdu version to learn that native language as well. This was also a translation of Kabishwar's text and it was done by Mazhar Ali Khan Vila alias Lutf, who was a poet and a translator working at Fort William College in Calcutta.[16]

THEMES

The *Vetala Panchavimshati* is a set of twenty-five extraordinary, curveball tales within a framework loosely held together by a ghostly trickster of a narrator. It has a goosebumps-inducing frame story about secret rituals to

---

[15]William Burckhardt Barker, *The Baitál Pachísí; or The Twenty-Five Tales of a Demon*, Hertford: Steven Austin, 1855.

[16]Rauf Parekh, 'Literary notes: Baital Pachcheese: an old Sanskrit legend and its Urdu versions', *Dawn*, 1 August 2022.

awaken dead bodies and a layered prologue about murder and deceit. The backdrop of the stories is a cremation ground, and their narrative arcs curve around the precipice of life and death. But, despite the foreboding atmosphere, the narratives are not sombre or weighty; they are light, capricious, and humorous, with unexpected plot twists and themes that explore life, love, sexuality, desires, relationships, and human behaviours. In most of the stories, the main cast of characters are lovers—men, handsome as Kamadeva, and women with faces as radiant as the moon—who fall passionately in love at first sight. Most often, this impulsive love proves to be cataclysmic; hence, the aftermath normally leads to the lovers' death. Therefore, many of these tales involve characters dying in unnatural ways: murder, suicide, self-immolation, sacrifice, etc. However, the tales do not focus on the grief or sadness of death; instead, the narrative question, in most of them, is about that crucial moment of heightened sensibility when life is on the brink of death.

PURPOSE OF THE RIDDLE QUESTIONS

The key narrative question defining the tales is posed as a riddle question that the vetala asks Raja Vikramaditya at the end of each story. Although the questions do not seem to demand it, the answers that the king gives are informed by his own understanding of dharma. This question-and-answer format may be just a literary device, but the context of dharma takes the *Vetala Panchavimshati* into the realm of wisdom literatures, notwithstanding its charnel and necromantical themes.

The tradition of riddles and riddle tales is as ancient as Vedic literatures. For instance, many of the metaphysical truths elucidated in the Upanishads are posed as riddling questions and answers between gurus and shishyas. The Mahabharata, too, has many such tales, mostly to expound dharma; for example, in the Yaksha–Yudhisthira incident in the 'Vana Parva', Dharmaraja, posing as a yaksha, asks Yudhisthira a series of questions to test his knowledge of dharma in exchange for his brothers' lives. Although the queries in these epical and scriptural texts are not quite the same as the story-end questions of the *Vetala Panchavimshati*, they serve a similar purpose. In the former, the riddle or question involves interrogative learning (mostly about metaphysical truths) to test the wisdom of the one who is questioned and, by proxy, to teach the one who is listening/reading. In the latter, the vetala does not seem to test Vikramaditya and only wants his engagement with the questions, irrespective of the rightness or wrongness of the response. However, these queries investigate the reader's grasp of dharma, making her/him think about the role that societal values play in human agency. They also upend our understanding of dharmic ethicality and make us acknowledge that dharma is ambiguous, often unknowable, and a matter of individual perception. Therefore, while the vetala's questions do not overtly plug dharma values, they force us to introspectively examine our own sense of right and wrong.

In terms of the narrative function of the questions: while structurally they essay the role of the denouement, they play out like the climax because they come as a surprise and unexpectedly change the reader's perspective of the narrative focus. The answers that Vikramaditya gives to the vetala are also surprising. Often, his responses do not meet our logic and our conventional morality; hence, they leave us bewildered and confused. This, perhaps, is the message of the book: there are rarely any straight and simple answers in life. Our actions have consequences that often leave us perplexed because we think we are in control, when, in fact, factors beyond our control are running the show. However, notwithstanding the hijack, one must continue to engage in thought and action; this is the diktat of life. Metaphorically, demonstrating this truth is the sword that the vetala hangs over Vikramaditya, threatening him that his head will explode into a thousand pieces if he knows the answer but remains silent. In other words, Vikramaditya is not required to know the *right* answer to these questions; he just needs to *engage* with the question and come up with an answer. Therefore, explicitly, the questions keep Vikramaditya involved in the stories, but implicitly, they are an advisement to the reader to never stop asking questions.

Hence, these riddle questions make the reader an active participant in the stories, directly connected with the vetala, just as Vikramaditya is. She/he eagerly awaits the question at the end of each story and then, like Vikramaditya, mulls over the response, even as Vikramaditya replies. This relationship with the vetala seduces the reader into yielding control to him, just as Vikramaditya does, because not only is the vetala the provocateur, but he is also the narrator of the tales. It is he who decides how the stories will play out and which questions will be posed, and it is also he who determines how and when the cycle of stories will end. His twenty-fourth tale is a story with an unanswerable question. Yet, like the sphinx sitting on the walls of Thebes, ready to kill those who cannot answer her questions, he warns Vikramaditya about the consequence of not answering—that his head will split into a thousand pieces. Vikramaditya does not know the answer and remains silent; however, he keeps walking towards the bargad, unfazed by the sword that is hanging over him. But his head does not shatter into a thousand pieces. Instead, impressed by his fearlessness and determination, the vetala rewards him. He reveals to him the true intention of the tantric yogi, thereby helping Vikramaditya turn the tables on the yogi and procure the sovereignty of the world.

On one level, the reader feels let down by the vetala's empty threat. But the vetala has been an unreliable narrator from the start, keeping the reader confused with his twisted tales, unbelievable situations, tangled relationships, and out-of-the-blue questions, and then chortling with glee at the futility of it all. It is not surprising then that the *Vetala Panchavimshati* is, sometimes, seen as 'a most clever collection of hoaxes from beginning to end'.[17] However, despite these cons and ambiguities, the *Vetala Panchavimshati* is, indeed, a nitishastra—a book of conduct—because it never loses sight of human behaviour.

THE AXIS OF THE BARGAD AND SHISHAM TREES

The setting of the *Vetala Panchavimshati* is the cremation ground and all the stories are told between two fixed points—the bargad tree on one end, under which the tantric yogi awaits the corpse that Vikramaditya will bring to him, and the shisham tree on the other end, from which the corpse hangs. Hence, the space between these two trees is clearly marked as an axis for the stories, but that is not all; these trees are also a symbolic conduit to facilitate the success of tantric aspirations.

The bargad tree is revered for numerous reasons in Hindu, Buddhist, and Jain cultures. It is considered divine,

[17]Willard Edward Farnham, 'The Contending Lovers', *PMLA*, Vol. 35, No. 3, 1920, p. 256.

because it is many-limbed: while its shoots grow upwards, it also puts down new roots, like feet. Hence, another name for the bargad is bahupada (multiple feet), which symbolizes constant mobility and growth. It is also called vata-vriksha (wide-spreading), because as it 'walks' with its multiple feet, its crown cover matches pace and the tree's canopy continues to expand, which is another symbol of perpetual growth. A bargad tree can, in fact, spread over several acres; for instance, the famous Thimmamma Marrimanu bargad in Anantapura, Andhra Pradesh, has 4,000 roots and a canopy of almost 5 acres.[18] Moreover, the bargad lives for centuries. Its longevity is proverbial and people believe that it knows the secrets of immortality. Hence, it is called nyagrodha kalpavriksha (the wish-fulfilling tree), or simply nyagrodha. All these metaphors of self-renewal, growth, and immortality represent the 'spiritual reality' of the undying soul; hence, the bargad 'is the botanical equivalent of the hermit'.[19]

The bargad is also associated with Yama, the Lord of Death, because it is believed to house in its branches supernatural spirits, like bhutas and pretas, and nature deities, like yakshas and yakshis. Not only are the latter associated with trees (and water bodies), but they are also attendants of Yama, whose other role is of Dharmaraja, the Lord of Justice. There are many Hindu myths that depict Yama assuming the form of a yaksha to interrogate people as Dharmaraja. This is the reason why another name for the bargad is yakshataru (the yaksha tree).

---

[18]Chris Griffiths, 'Thimmamma Marrimanu: The world's largest single tree canopy', *BBC,* 20 February 2020.

[19]Trupti More, Vijaya Valhe, 'SYMBOLIC SIGNIFICANCE OF SACRED *NYAGRODHA* TREE WORSHIP IN INDIAN RELIGION AND TRADITIONS', *Bulletin of the Deccan College, Post Graduate and Research Institute,* Vol. 80, October 2020, p. 151.

Yama also has two dogs, Sharvara and Shyama, that wander in cremation grounds, shepherding the dead to him. That is why bargads are often planted near cremation grounds.[20] All together, these symbolic reasons make the bargad an important tree in tantrism and, thus, a fitting spot for the yogi to receive the dead body and create his altar.

On the other hand, the shisham (also called shimshipa) tree, in which the corpse hangs, is known more for its usefulness than for its association with the occult or metaphysics; however, it, too, is symbolically connected to what the tantric yogi hopes to accomplish. Shisham wood is tough and hardy; hence, it is often used in the construction of door and window frames, furniture, and other items of household and commercial use. Moreover, it is a tall tree with sturdy branches that can withstand the harshest elements of nature, including the shenanigans of a vetala. Most importantly, the shisham is, virtually, a non-decaying tree, resistant to degeneration. This is especially significant because tantric shava-sadhana (meditation of the corpse) calls for a whole and undecayed body. Hence, Kshantisheela, the tantric yogi of *Vetala Panchavimshati,* could not have chosen a more appropriate tree to hang the corpse, because, with the right tantric rituals, the shisham can alchemize the dead body with its inherent potency.

The *Vetala Panchavimshati* is, thus, staged in this liminal space between the two tree poles of immortality and the undead. And the medium who knows how to navigate this space, connect the two ends, and unlock the secret to the supernatural powers that the yogi seeks is the vetala.

---

[20]Ibid.

WHO IS VETALA?

Those of us who grew up listening to or reading Vikram-and-Vetala stories have a mental image of the vetala. For some of us, that image derives from the popular television series, *Vikram Aur Betaal,* that aired on Doordarshan in 1985–86. In this series, the vetala is shown as an old man with scraggly white hair and an evil grin under a long, witchy nose, riding on Vikram's muscular, bare back. For other readers of a certain age, who are from the early *Chandamama* generation, the idea of the vetala is based on the image that was created by *Chandamama*'s famous illustrator, Karatholuvu Chandrasekaran Sivasankaran. In this image, Vikram, wearing an elegant red angarakha, is holding a naked sword in one hand and a limp body on his shoulder with the other, as he makes his way through piles of bones and skulls. There is no vetala in the image, but his absence is what makes his presence palpable; it is there in the way Vikram looks over his shoulder, his handsome, moustachioed face deadpan, but his eyes wary and watchful. Prior to *Chandamama*'s iconic image, the vetala that readers knew was from illustrations in the translated versions of *Vetala Panchavimshati* by Western scholars. These depictions were normally of a demonic creature from Western myth and legend, such as the 1870 illustrations by Ernest Griset for Richard Burton's *Vikram and the Vampire*. As the title itself suggests, the vetala in this adaptation was shown as a vulturish gargoyle with winged legs and a forked tail.

In his earliest known avatar, in the *Kathasaritsagara*, the vetala is quite a bit different from any of these depictions. He is a chimera: dark-complexioned and very tall, with a neck like a camel's, face like an elephant's, feet like a bull's, eyes like an owl's, ears like a donkey's.[21] (This is not the vetala that Vikramaditya himself encounters; it is a different vetala, who, another hero, Mrigankadatta, meets in a similar environment.)

So, what does a vetala really look like? As a matter of fact, all the above descriptions fit vetala, because he is a shapeshifter. He is also sly yet playful, childlike yet wise, and helpful yet dangerous—in other words, a perfect paradigmatic Jungian archetype of a trickster: a liminal, ambiguous, paradoxical shapeshifter who 'hints at a secret inner relation of evil to good and vice versa'.[22] Also, 'just when we've decided he's a villain, he does something heroic'.[23] But, like most tricksters, vetala likes to put people on trial, as he does Raja Vikramaditya. He puts the king on a hamster wheel and watches him run—repeatedly climbing the tree, taking down the corpse, attempting to bring it to the yogi, and returning to the tree to do it all over again. In the process, he also tells the king amusing, convoluted yet thought-provoking stories, seemingly to lessen his tedium, but, more so, to make him think. At the end of each story, he threatens to cause the king's head to explode if he does not answer his question. And then, in yet another surprising move, after the twenty-fourth story, he saves the king's life and rewards him with everything the yogi had desired for himself.

Hence, despite his threats, the vetala in the *Vetala Panchavimshati* turns out to be harmless. But this is not the case with all vetalas. In tantrism, a vetala is a dangerous being who can prove fatal at any time. The process of gaining control of

---

[21]*Kathasaritsagara*, Shri Jatashankara Jha and Shri Prafullachandra Ojha 'Mukta' (trans.), Vol. 3, Patna: Bihar Rashtrabhasha Parishad, 2000.

[22]Jung quoted in Ilona Błocian, 'The Archetype of the Trickster in the Writings of C.G. Jung', *Studia Religiologica*, Vol. 53, No. 3, 2020, p. 23.

[23]Tim Callahan, 'Devil, Trickster and Fool', *Mythlore*, Vol. 17, No. 4 (66), 1991, p. 29.

the vetala through vetala siddhi is long and difficult, requiring absolute dedication and exactitude. If a preparatory ritual is not performed accurately, the vetala can destroy the aspiring tantric. And once the aspirant has the vetala under control, he can be employed for evil purposes (or good depending on the intention of the controller). A good example of this is in a *Kathasaritsagara* tale: Vikramaditya summons Agnishikha, a vetala he controls, and commands him to destroy a kapalika yogi who is trying to kidnap the beautiful Madanamanjari. Agnishikha enters a dead body and grabbing the kapalika, flings him to the ground, smashing him to bits.[24]

Vetalas are associated with Shiva's Kalabhairava form, who is variously described with fangs and dreadlocks, and a face as dark as Kali, wearing either serpents or skull garlands around his neck. The myth that explains Shiva's transformation into Bhairava is as follows: once, on Mount Meru, all the sages ask Brahma who among the gods is supreme and unchanging. Brahma states that it is he himself, since he is Hiranyagarbha, the golden womb, and all things are created from him. Brahma's response infuriates Vishnu, because he considers himself supreme, since it is he who dreams the world into existence. Thus, Vishnu confronts Brahma and the two begin to argue. Unable to reconcile their dispute, the two gods then go to the Vedas and ask them who they think is the supreme being. The Vedas name Rudra Shiva. Both Brahma and Vishnu scoff at this idea. 'That ash-smeared outsider, who wears snakes for garments?' they mock. 'How can he be supreme?' Suddenly, before them, a great fire erupts, filling the space between heaven and earth. In the flames is a man—Nilalohita—holding

[24]*Kathasaritsagara*, Shri Jatashankara Jha and Shri Prafullachandra Ojha 'Mukta' (trans.), Vol. 3, Patna: Bihar Rashtrabhasha Parishad, 2000.

a trident. On his forehead is a third eye, snakes range around his neck and waist, and a crescent moon shines in his locks. Seeing him, Brahma's fifth head jeers, 'In the past you were born from my forehead. I called you Rudra, because you cried.' Angered by Brahma's mockery, Shiva transforms his own being into Bhairava and, naming him Kalabhairava (he who controls time and he whom time itself fears), commands him to cut off Brahma's fifth head for its arrogance. In return, Shiva promises overlordship of his own city, Kashi, which is the ultimate liminality of time, since life and death perpetually meet in its cremation grounds. Thus, Kalabhairava is given suzerainty over both life and death. Kalabhairava cuts off Brahma's fifth head with his left thumb nail, but, with this act, he commits the sin of killing a brahmin; therefore, brahmanicide attaches to him in the form of Brahma's skull stuck to his hand. To help Kalabhairava atone for his sin, Shiva advises him to carry this skull (kapalika) in his hand till he gets to Kashi, where it will fall off by itself. Kalabhairava wanders the earth for twelve years, receiving alms in the skull in his hand. Finally, when he reaches Kashi, the kapala (skull) falls to the ground. That site where the skull is released, along with Kalabhairava's sin, is called Kapalamochana (the release of the kapala).[25] This myth is told in various Puranas with slight variations, but the core is the same in all of them—that Shiva transforms into the terrible and fierce form of Kalabhairava to cut off the head of arrogance and egoity, and that all sins, even those as grievous as brahmanicide, can be expiated with penance.

Kalabhairava is attended by shadowy, ghoulish creatures, such as bhutas, pretas, and pishachas. The former two are

[25]*The Śiva-Purāṇa: Ancient Indian Tradition and Mythology*, J. L. Shastri (ed.), Vol. 3, Delhi: Motilal Banarsidass Publishers, 1960.

spectral remnants of people who have died: bhutas are ghosts of the deceased who were cremated but, for some reason, are still wandering the earthly plane; pretas are wandering souls of people who died a violent death or are yet to receive obsequial rites and hence cannot move on. Both are sometimes noxious and can harm people. Pishachas, on the other hand, are not remnants of humans or residual energy from deceased beings; therefore, they have no way of moving on. Neither do they belong to this world nor to the world of ancestors. They are spirits of nature that exist in nature and feed on human flesh. Vetalas are also spirits of nature; they do not normally eat human flesh, but they often inhabit human corpses, because they like to form 'constructive relationships with human beings' that sometimes prove dangerous.[26] Most of these relationships are forged by magic and alchemy, and promise extraordinary powers to anyone who can gain control over them. Hence, they are often sought by ascetics, especially practitioners of tantra, who spend their lives completing the arduous sadhana and performing various macabre rituals to acquire vetala siddhi, even at the risk of the vetala turning on them and destroying them.

Vetala sadhana is part of Vamachara tantra, also known as the left-hand path, which is a heterodoxical pursuit that involves unconventional and, often, extreme practices. It is common to Shaiva, Shakta, Buddhist, and Jain traditions. However, the rites that are described in *Vetala Panchavimshati* are equivalent to those customary in the Shaiva–Shakta tradition of tantra, which includes shava-sadhana. In this sadhana, Shiva, who is Mahakala (Great Time) and the Lord

---

[26]Michael Walter, 'Of Corpses and Gold: Materials for the Study of the Vetāla and the Ro langs', *The Tibet Journal*, Vol. 29, No. 2, Summer 2004, p. 14.

of Death, is propriated, but in its culmination it is the Goddess that manifests and fulfils the yogi's desire. Most often, this Goddess is the ferocious Mahakali, the consort of Mahakala, whom *Tantrasara*, a sixteenth-century Shakta text, describes as 'dark as soot, always living in the cremation ground. Her eyes are pink, her hair dishevelled, her body gaunt and fearful. In her left hand she holds a cup filled with wine and meat, and in her right hand she holds a freshly cut human head'.[27]

Vetala sadhana and shava-sadhana were prevalent in medieval India, and they are still practised by certain ascetic sects, such as the Shaiva Aghoris. The ritual process of attaining this knowledge is mostly derived from the seventh-century text *Brahmayamala Tantra* or *Pichumata*. The rituals that Kshantisheela, the tantric yogi of *Vetala Panchavimshati,* performs to bring the vetala under his control are very similar to what is described in this text.

> The ritual takes place on the 8th or 14th day of the dark fortnight, in a cremation ground. The sadhaka's valorous assistant fetches him the corpse of someone who has been hanged or impaled.... The sadhaka shaves the corpse completely, washes it with perfumes and myrobalan, and treats it with reverence.... Then he performs various preparatory rituals, such as the appropriation of the ground, the projecting of the mantras into his own body and into the corpse....
>
> The corpse should be laid out with its head towards the south. The sadhaka should prepare a seat on the corpse's heart and sit down on it, facing south. Then

[27]David Kinsley, 'KĀLĪ: Blood and Death Out of Place', *Devī Goddess of India*, John Stratton Hawley and Donna Marie Wolff (eds.), Berkeley: University of California Press, 1996, p. 77.

> he should kindle a fire in the open mouth of the corpse into which he should perform the homa sacrifice.... Then smoke resembling a cloud arises from the mouth of the corpse, and the sadhaka should offer argha guest-water....
>
> A huge flame will arise from the mouth of the corpse, shining like a thousand suns, as if burning up the three worlds. Then the tongue of the corpse will emerge greedily towards the adept, who should cut it with a razor or a knife kept at hand, before it touches him. If he fails to do so he will be devoured. As he grasps the tongue, it will turn into a shining sword in his hand.[28]

The yogi in *Vetala Panchavimshati* is able to accomplish only the initial preparatory rituals, because he is interrupted by the vetala, who transposes the sacrifice and the sacrificer; therefore, instead of Kshantisheela cutting Vikramaditya's head, Vikramaditya cuts Kshantisheela's head. However, this switching of aspirants makes no difference to the dark forces of alchemy; they are not concerned with who concludes the twelve years of sadhana and who is sacrificed. All that matters to them is that the powers are properly propitiated with a fresh corpse, perfect rituals, accurate mantras, and a sacrifice. Thus, it is assumed that Vikramaditya completes the remaining rituals, and since he is the one who ultimately offers the sacrifice (of the yogi), he is the winner. Hence, it is he who finally controls the vetala. Ergo, it is he who receives all the powers for which the yogi had built his tantric altar. What is implied by this switch is that if the yogi had gained

---

[28]Csaba Dezső, 'ENCOUNTERS WITH "VETĀLAS" STUDIES ON FABULOUS CREATURES I', *Acta Orientalia Academiae Scientiarum Hungaricae*, Vol. 63, No. 4, 2010, pp. 394–96.

control of the vetala and siddhis, he would have used the immense power for personal gain or for nefarious purposes. But Vikramaditya, being the monarch that he is, will employ the power of vetala siddhi for the welfare of people.

Thus, ultimately, the *Vetala Panchavimshati* is a glorification of the great Raja Vikramaditya, who 'has been shining brighter than the sun for eons', and he will be celebrated for 'as long as the moon, sun, and earth remain fixed in their places' (from 'How the Story Ends' in this retelling).

Kathamukha

Raja Gandharvasena of Dhara Nagara had four wives and six sons. Each of his sons was highly intelligent, valorous, and worthy of being his successor. After he passed away, his eldest son, Shanka, was crowned king. Shanka was competent and just, and he ruled for several years, but then his brother Vikrama assassinated him and usurped the throne. Vikrama was an astute ruler and courageous warrior, and, within a few years of his reign, he expanded the kingdom over the entirety of Jambudvipa, creating an unfaltering sovereignty that defined an era.

After ruling for many years, Raja Vikrama felt the desire to visit those faraway lands that sailors and traders talked about. Thus, handing over the governance of the kingdom to his younger brother Bharthari, he donned the garb of a wandering ascetic and embarked on his travels.

Bharthari ruled Dhara Nagara with diligence and care. Then, an incident occurred which forced Vikrama to return home. In Dhara Nagara was a brahmin who lived on alms and spent his days meditating on the Goddess. One day, when he was deep in meditation, a fruit dropped into his lap. The startled brahmin looked around to see where it could have come from. There were no fruit trees where he was sitting, and there did not seem to be anyone around. Then, a celestial voice came from the sky: 'I am Devi, O Brahmin, and this is the fruit of immortality. Eat it and be immortal!' The brahmin quickly got up and thanked the Goddess. Then, wrapping the fruit in his shawl, he rushed home to his wife. 'Look what the Goddess has given me, dear wife,' he said to her excitedly. 'It's a fruit of immortality. Bring me a knife and I'll cut it in half. You eat one piece and I'll eat the other; that way we'll both become immortal.'

Instead of jumping with joy, the brahmin's wife began to wail. 'Oh, what injustice!' she cried. 'This is how the gods reward us for our devotion. They want to make us immortal so that there will be no end to our suffering. We are beggars and we'll remain beggars forever. I'd rather die. At least, death will liberate us from this life of misery.'

'I didn't think about it this way,' the brahmin replied. 'When the Goddess gave me the fruit, I willingly received it and felt excited about becoming immortal, but your words have made me realize how reckless that would be. What is your advice then, Wife? What should we do with this fruit?'

'Go and give it to the raja in exchange for money. Tell him how extraordinary this fruit is and ask him for a big sum. Besides, think how useful this fruit will be if our kind and caring raja eats it. His long life will benefit the whole world. What will *we* do with immortality?'

Taking his wife's advice, the brahmin went to the king and presented him the fruit. 'Maharaj,' he said, 'this is the fruit of immortality. If you eat it, you'll become immortal and remain young and healthy forever. It'll give me great happiness if you accept it. In exchange, I ask only that you give me an appropriate sum of money.'

Raja Bharthari accepted the fruit and gave the brahmin one lakh gold coins. Then he went to the women's palace and presented the fruit to his queen, whom he loved very much. 'Dearest,' he said, 'I want you to have this. It's the fruit of immortality. Whoever eats this will remain young forever. I want you to never lose your youth and beauty.'

'What a precious fruit!' the queen exclaimed. 'Dear

husband, I'll happily eat it, but I must take a bath first to purify myself. Why don't you go back to court and come and see me later?'

As soon as the king left, the queen summoned her lover, who was the kingdom's chief security officer, and offered him the fruit. The security officer, in turn, loved a courtesan, so he brought the fruit to her. The courtesan was a farsighted, prudent woman. When she received the fruit, she began to think what could be its best possible use that would bring her long-term benefits. 'Why don't I give this extraordinary fruit to the king,' she said to herself. 'That'll put me in his good graces and allow me to draw upon his favours for as long as I live.' Hence, the courtesan went to court and respectfully laid the fruit at Raja Bharthari's feet. 'Maharaj,' she said, 'this is the fruit of immortality. Whoever eats it will become immortal and remain young forever. Please accept this gift from me.'

Bharthari was shocked to see the fruit, but he accepted it without a word and gave the courtesan a large sum of money for it. Then he sat on his throne, thinking about how the material world of relationships and desires was as tormenting as the suffering and tortures of hell. 'It's far better to renounce this world and dedicate oneself to the worship of the Divine,' he said to himself and decided to live the rest of his life as a renunciate. However, before putting on the clothes of a sanyasi, he went to his queen one last time and confronted her. 'What did you do with the fruit I gave you?' he asked her.

'I ate it, Maharaj,' she replied innocently.

Bharthari reached inside his shawl and brought out the fruit.

The queen's face blanched. 'Ho...how...did you get that?' she stammered.

Without another word, Bharthari returned to his room and asked a servant to wash the fruit. Then he sat down and ate the whole thing. After that, he removed his kingly ornaments and garments, changed into a simple, saffron dhoti and shawl, and left the palace to go and live in the forest.

When Indra learned that Raja Bharthari had gone to the forest and left Dhara Nagara without a king, he was deeply concerned. He quickly dispatched a big and powerful danava to the kingdom, commanding him to guard it with his life. This danava, Prithvipala, began to watch over Dhara Nagara day and night, making sure it was protected from spies and infiltrators.

In the meantime, word about Bharthari's renunciation reached Raja Vikrama and, fearing for his kingdom, he immediately left for Dhara Nagara. It was around midnight when he arrived at the city gate and there, he was accosted by Prithvipala.

'Stop right there!' the danava called. 'Who are you and what is your business in Dhara Nagara?'

'Who are you and how dare you stop me from entering my city?' Vikrama replied. 'I'm Raja Vikrama and this is my city.'

'I'm Danava Prithvipala. Indradeva has sent me to protect this city. If you truly are Raja Vikrama, then prove it to me by fighting me. If you win, I'll let you enter.'

Tightening his kamarbanda, the raja faced the danava, who charged at him with a roar. The two fought for many hours, grunting in pain and shouting expletives, as the air around them filled with sounds of slamming fists, slapping skin, and breaking bones. They were equally matched, even though the danava was three times the size of Raja Vikrama. Finally, with a surprise manoeuvre, Vikrama put the danava in a headlock and, flinging him to the ground, mounted his massive chest.

Prithvipala did not struggle to get out of the headlock, nor did he make any attempt to dislodge Vikrama; instead, he said to him, 'O Raja, I can give you the boon of life.'

Vikrama laughed. 'Are you insane? You're on the ground. My muscled arm is at your neck. I could kill you this instant; yet *you* are offering *me* the boon of life?'

'You may have brought me down, but no one can beat Kala. I can save you from the lethal strike of Great Time,' the danava said. 'Not only that. If you listen to what I have to say, you can become a Chakravarti Raja and rule the world.'

Intrigued by the danava's words, Raja Vikrama released him. 'Speak!' he commanded, and the danava began to tell him a story:

'Your father, Raja Gandharvasena, was a generous and charitable king, but one night he made the error of letting his kingly pride override his good sense. That night, he was walking in the forest, when he saw a strange sight: an ascetic was hanging upside down from a tree. Curious to know why he was doing this, the raja stood and watched him for a while. The man neither moved nor spoke, but he was clearly alive, and it appeared that he was living only on air, without any other sustenance.

"O Yogi," the raja called out to him. "Why are you hanging upside down from a tree?"

The yogi didn't respond, so your father asked him again. However, it seemed that the man was completely oblivious to the king's presence. Angered by his disregard, your father returned to the palace, determined to teach the yogi a lesson. Therefore, the next day, he declared in court that he would give one lakh gold coins to anyone who brought this yogi to his court.

Everyone heard the declaration, but no one had the courage to step forward and accept the challenge, because this was not just an impossible task; it was also a dangerous one. Clearly, that yogi was highly advanced in his tapasya and had accumulated enough mental power to destroy anyone who dared to disturb him.

In Gandharvasena's court was a courtesan—Vasantasena. She was a skilled tactician and a stunning beauty. "Maharaj," she announced, "I'll bring you this yogi."

"I know you are capable of doing this, Vasantasena," Gandharvasena said to her. "But, be warned, this yogi's resolve is unshakable."

"Maharaj, a woman is like a pot of butter and a man is like a live coal. When the fire in him melts a woman, she becomes irresistible to him. Please trust me when I say that he'll not be able to resist me. I promise you that not only will I bring this man to court, but also when he comes, he'll be carrying our son on his shoulders."

The raja applauded Vasantasena. "Your beauty can entice even the gods; that yogi is but a mere mortal. I look forward to the day when you'll achieve this goal. I wish you success."

Leaving the court, Vasantasena went home to beautify herself. She bathed in sandalwood-scented water and draped herself in seductive clothes of transparent fabric that barely concealed her womanliness. She also donned gold necklaces that drew attention to her ample bosom, a gold belt that cinched her curvaceous waist, and dangling earrings that enhanced her long neck. Then she applied a soft, dewy, pink colour from the extract of roses on her lips and cheeks, red hue from vermillion on her feet and hands, and black kohl in her eyes. Once she was satisfied with her appearance, she called her charioteer and had him drive her to the forest.

Going in the direction that the raja had given, she soon saw the tree from which the yogi was hanging. Telling the charioteer to stop at a distance from the tree, she stepped down from the chariot and walked towards the yogi. It was exactly as the king had described—he was hanging from a thick, leafy branch, with his head down and feet up, completely still except for the slight rise and fall of his chest. She noticed that while his body was lean, it was not gaunt, even though he lived only on air. She also saw that he was completely disengaged with the world around him; his eyes were half-shut, and his gaze was steady and inward-looking. But as she stood observing him, she noticed that every time he breathed out, his lips parted slightly. Seeing that, a plan formed in her mind. Returning to the city, she put together the items she would need and went back to the forest with two of her men. She had the men construct a small, makeshift hut of bark and hay, and then sent them away with the chariot. Inside the hut, she started a cooking fire and made a pot of halwa and put it in a large bowl. Bringing it to the tree, she sat down near the yogi's head, and, scooping a mouthful of the halwa with the tips of her fingers and thumb, she waited. As the yogi opened his lips to exhale, she slipped the halwa into his mouth. The yogi's mouth worked instinctively, his tongue savouring the sweet, buttery taste. When he opened his lips again, the courtesan slipped in another mouthful. In this way, bit by bit, Vasantasena fed him all the halwa she had made. Then she went back to the hut and prepared more. For two days, Vasantasena made the yogi taste the sweetness of halwa, and, on the third morning, he opened his eyes and looked directly at her. Then, turning himself right side up, he planted his feet on the ground and stood in front of her. "Who are you and what are you doing here?" he asked.

"I'm a celestial woman," the courtesan replied. "I was deep in meditation in heaven when I felt a sudden urge to come to earth, to this forest. And here I am."

The ascetic looked at her from head to toe and, as his eyes traced her alluring, barely concealed body, he felt an overwhelming surge of lust. "Please stay with me?" he begged. "I'm in love with you."

"I live among the gods," Vasantasena replied. "But I'll stay with you, because the power of your meditation has pulled me to earth. What is your name?"

"Valkalashana," he said.

"Will you come with me, Valkalashana?" she asked. "I'll take you to the hut that I have built for myself in this forest."

"I'll happily go with you wherever you take me. But why are you staying in a hut? Let me give you a palace," the yogi said. "My tapasya has given me the ability to acquire whatever I desire, just by thinking it." Then he closed his eyes and, at once, conjured a beautiful, fully furnished palace in the middle of the forest.

The two of them began to live together in that palace with Vasantasena catering to the yogi from morning till night. Every day, she also cooked him a meal of six delicious dishes and fed him with her own hands. The very first time she made him this food, full of enticing aromas and addictive tastes, he gave up living on air. Soon, from a lean ascetic who had renounced the world, he began to transform into a well-built and handsome worldly man who enjoyed earthly pleasures, including making love to the courtesan, who he believed to be a celestial woman. Shortly thereafter, Vasantasena became pregnant, as she had hoped, and, in due time, she gave birth to a boy. With the birth of his son, the yogi gave up the last vestiges of his renunciate life and became fully immersed in the love of his son. All day he would play with him in the forest, delighting in his childish antics and lisping talk.

When the boy turned one, Vasantasena said to the man

who had once been a yogi, "Let's leave the forest and move to a city so that our son can learn how to live in this world. Besides, living in a forest is so dangerous. I fear that a wild animal will kill our son if I so much as take my eyes off him."

"Where shall we go, dearest?" he asked.

And she replied, "When I was in heaven, I heard about the city of Dhara. I've heard that even the gods favour it, because it's very conducive to good living. I've also heard that its raja is dharma-abiding and he is welcoming towards guests."

The very next morning, Vasantasena and Valkalashana left for Dhara, with the latter proudly carrying his son on his shoulders. As soon as they entered Dhara's court, Raja Gandharvasena saw them. "Look!" he said to his courtiers. "Isn't this Courtesan Vasantasena? She had promised to bring me the hanging yogi with their son riding on his shoulders, and here she is."

"Yes, indeed, Maharaj," the courtiers replied. "She has kept her word. That appears to be the yogi walking beside her and he's carrying their boy on his shoulders."

"I pity the man," Gandharvasena said with a smile. "His tapasya couldn't reach completion. He was forced to surrender to the wiles of our beautiful Vasantasena."

The courtiers laughed. "Maharaj, what tapasya can withstand a face as lustrous as the shining moon, a gait as supple as a she-elephant, and loins as vigorous as a proud lion? Only Vasantasena could have curbed the arrogance of the yogi. No one else could have done it."

Hearing this exchange between the king and his courtiers, Valkalashana stopped short. It dawned on him that the woman he had thought to be a heavenly being was merely a clever courtesan whom the king had sent to destroy his tapasya. Enraged at the deception staged by Raja Gandharvasena and Vasantasena, and even more angry at his own gullibility, Valkalashana pulled down the boy from his shoulders and, holding him by the ankles, violently flung him on the floor. The child's body came apart—limbs, head, and torso flying in different directions. His head landed in the queen's palace, his torso fell in a potter's house, and his feet dropped in an oil merchant's house.

That very day, three women conceived: the queen, the potter's wife, and the oil merchant's wife. In due time, all three women gave birth to boys on the same day and at the same time.'

'The gist of the matter is this,' Prithvipala said to Raja Vikrama. 'Three boys were born in the same city, in the same lunar mansion, in the same division of the great ecliptic circle, and in the same period of time, and they all grew up in this city. You are one of them; you were born to the king, the second was born to the oil merchant, and the third was born to the potter. When you were born, your father asked the royal astrologer to draw up your natal chart. After calculating the time and position of the planets in your chart, the astrologer informed your father that your birth was very auspicious, because five key planets were at their pinnacle: Sun in Aries, Moon in Taurus, Mercury in Virgo, Venus is Pisces, and Jupiter in Cancer. "This portends greatness, Maharaj," he said and named you Vikramaditya, the Sun of Valour. "I see in this boy's chart that he will demonstrate valour at a very young age," he told your father. But he also informed him about the other two boys that were born in the same planetary configuration. "All three are born for greatness," he stated. "However, among the three, only one can achieve greatness. Therefore, that one will kill the other two and rule the earth."

Similarly, when the potter and oilman had their sons' natal charts prepared, they, too, were told, "Three boys were born in the same city, in the same lunar mansion, in the same division of the great ecliptic circle, and in the same period of time. All three are born for greatness. But among the three, only one can achieve greatness. Therefore, that one will kill the other two and rule the earth."

In due time, you and the other two boys grew up. You were crowned king, after your brother Shanka died, and the other two assumed their fathers' professions. The oil merchant's son was quite satisfied with his life. His business was successful, and he had money enough to live a comfortable life. However, the potter's son could hardly eke out a living, no matter how hard he worked. One day, as he sat bemoaning his fate, he recalled the astrologer's prediction and asked himself, "Why am I working so hard at the potter's wheel, when all I have to do to rule the world is kill the oil merchant's son and the king?"

That day, the potter's son devised a plan and began to work towards its realization. He started by courting a friendship with the oil merchant's son. Then he began inviting him to his house, giving him gifts, and constantly telling him how much he treasured his friendship. In this way, he soon gained his trust. One day, he said to the oil merchant's son, "I have to perform a fire ritual for my dead father's soul and for that I must gather firewood. Will you come with me to the forest to help me collect the wood?"

"Of course," said the oil merchant's son and, without a moment's hesitation, accompanied his friend to the forest. The potter's son led the merchant's son deep into the woodland, where the trees grew densely and very little light penetrated. There, he threw a noose around his neck and strangled him, and then, tying his feet with a rope, he strung him up, upside down, from a branch of a shisham tree. After that, he returned home via a secret path that only he knew. However, somehow, people got wind of his crime and threatened to report him; therefore, he fled the land.'

'O King,' Prithvipala the danava continued, 'this man who murdered his friend, who was born in the same planetary configuration as you and shares your fate, is now on the lookout for an opportunity to kill you as well. Once he accomplishes that, the destiny of ruling over the earth will be his alone, and that is what he seeks. Escape him, if you can. And know that if you do manage to escape his dark designs, you'll not only retain your kingdom and rule for a long time, but you'll also become a Chakravarti Raja. However, all this is only possible if you can circumvent the plan he has for you. This is my warning to you and it's the boon of life I promised.' Saying this, the danava vanished.

Unperturbed by Prithvipala's revelation but equipped with prescience about the intention of the potter's son, Raja Vikrama entered his city. Word of his arrival spread rapidly and with the first light of the sun, courtiers and prominent citizens began to stream into the court to welcome him back and felicitate him. Raja Vikrama declared a week of festivities throughout the kingdom and Dhara Nagara became immersed in celebrations. Jubilated at the return of their beloved king, people strung marigold flowers in the streets and decorated their home with colourful banners. They sang and danced from sunrise to sunset, while bards roamed in market squares eulogizing the king in story and song. This is how Raja Vikramaditya began the new era of his reign.

How the Story Begins

The glorious Raja Vikramaditya shone brighter than a million suns when he sat on his lion throne embedded with jewels that sparkled and glistened like a thousand rays of sunlight. He was as handsome as Kamadeva, as majestic as Indra, and as benevolent as Shiva. The furious passion he aimed at his enemies was as fiery as Mahadeva's pralaya, which brings an end to the world. In the execution of justice, his legend was so great that his very name was equated with Dharmaraja. And in the matters of law, his deliberations were cited even in Indra's court. He never digressed from the decrees set down in the shastras and was held up as an example by people who were wise and virtuous. He was magnanimous towards all his subjects and fair in all his dealings, even towards his enemies, who threw down their weapons just at the mention of his name. He was valorous, magnificent, and awesome. If ever there was a king who could be called the zenith of kingship in the world, it was Raja Vikramaditya.

Every morning, when Vikramaditya held court, with his exemplary ministers in attendance, any citizen who desired to see the king was allowed to enter. One day, a kapalika yogi came to visit the king. His name was Kshantisheela, which means, 'one who has patience'. Approaching the lion throne, he held out a small fruit as a gift. Vikramaditya greeted the ascetic with due respect and, accepting the fruit, handed it to his minister of gifts. The ascetic bowed and left without saying a word. The following morning he returned and, again, gifted a fruit to the raja, who respectfully accepted it and passed it to his minister. In this way, for twelve years, every day, the ascetic came to Vikramaditya's court and gave him a fruit, which the raja handed to his minister of gifts.

Then, one morning, as the ascetic placed the fruit in the raja's hand and the raja held it out to his minister, the fruit slipped from his fingers and fell to the floor. The raja's pet monkey, who was sitting on his shoulder, saw the rolling fruit and leapt on it. When he put it between his teeth and cracked it open, something fell out of it and clattered on the floor. Everyone was flabbergasted to see that it was a brilliant, magnificent jewel.

'Oh, what a jewel!' the courtiers exclaimed.

The raja, too, was astounded to see it, and, when it dawned on him that each of the fruits he had received from the ascetic for twelve years probably held a similar jewel, he could hardly contain his excitement. Turning to the minister, he asked him urgently, 'What have you done with all the fruits I've been handing to you?'

'Maharaj, I've been dropping the fruits into the storeroom of the treasure house through the trellis of a window,' the trepidatious minister replied.

'Go and see what's become of them,' the king commanded.

The minister ran to the storeroom and when he returned, his eyes were still popping out. 'Maharaj,' he said to the king in amazement, 'there's a glittering mountain in the treasury. In the pile of rotting fruit, there are thousands of gems.'

'Aha!' Raja Vikramaditya exclaimed, thrilled at having accumulated so much wealth without even knowing it. However, he was also very curious to know why the ascetic had given him this fortune. Therefore, the next morning when the ascetic walked into the court and held out the fruit to him, he refused to take it. 'I'll only accept this if you tell me why you've been gifting me such priceless gems every day for twelve years,' he said.

'May we talk in private, Maharaj?' the ascetic requested. 'I'd rather not disclose it in public. You must have heard what the wise say: if a secret is heard by six ears, it no longer remains a secret; heard by four ears, it can remain hidden; however, if heard by just two ears, not even the Creator knows what it is.'

Vikramaditya gestured to his personal attendants to take the ascetic to a private room and joined him there. 'Now tell me the reason,' he demanded. 'What is it that you want to say to me and what are you hoping to gain from giving me those gems?'

'Maharaj, I've been doing tapasya for twelve years, practising a strict discipline of austerities in preparation for a very special ritual by which I'll obtain eight sidhis. These will enable me to become as minute as an atom, as big as a mountain, as light as air, and as heavy as rock. I'll also be able to make myself invisible, have control over the will of others, fulfil all my desires, and be the lord of the world. However, to perform this difficult ritual and bring it to fruition, I need the help of a valorous man like you.'

'Tell me in detail how I can help you?' the raja asked.

'On the fourteenth night of the waning moon that falls just before the beginning of the dark half of the month, come to the cremation ground on the bank of river Shipra, before the night descends. I'll meet you there and tell you what I need you to do.'

'How will I find you?'

'I'll be sitting under the bargad tree.'

'All right,' promised the king. 'I'll be there.'

On the evening of the fourteenth day of the waning moon, the brave Raja Vikramaditya tightened the strap of his baldric, slipped his sword into the sheath hanging by his side, and covered himself with a dark blue shawl. Then, pulling the shawl over his head, he left the palace by a secret gate and headed towards the cremation ground. At the entrance of the ground, he stood for a moment, peering at the vast expanse of ghoulish darkness, before walking with resolute steps in the direction of the bargad tree. Around him night birds screeched, and bhutas and pretas wailed, while the air sighed and wafts of breeze brushed past like death's breath. Here and there cremation fires sizzled with melting flesh and crackled with remnants of brains and entrails. Bleached skulls and long bones lay strewn everywhere, as though this was Death's playground. Ignoring every shape, shadow, and sound, Vikramaditya kept walking till he saw the bargad tree and under it the ascetic, who was sitting with legs crossed and eyes closed, muttering mantras.

'Sanyasi,' the raja called him, 'I'm here. Tell me what you need me to do.'

The tantric yogi's eyelids lifted and he smiled at the king, his teeth a sudden flash of white. 'You've kept your promise, O Raja. I'm grateful for that. Not many men would have had the courage to come here. The task I have for you is a simple one, but it requires a fearless heart.'

'I'm listening, Sanyasi. Tell me what it is.'

'Go south. After about half a yojana, you'll see a shisham tree. Hanging from a branch of that tree is a dead body. I want you to bring that body to me.'

'All right,' Raja Vikramaditya said and started walking in the southerly direction, using the glow of the burning pyres to find his way. More skulls, limbs, and body parts, some still covered with rotting flesh, lined his path, like garlands celebrating Bhairava, the destructive avatar of the Lord of Annihilation. Soon, he came to the shisham tree and saw that from one of its high branches, a corpse was hanging by a rope tied around its ankles. It looked like the man had only recently died, because the body showed no signs of decay. Without a moment's hesitation, Vikramaditya quickly climbed the tree and cut the rope with his sword. The body dropped with a thud, but just as it hit the ground, it cried out, as though in pain. Vikramaditya jumped off the tree, happy at the discovery that the man was still alive. However, as he reached a hand to touch him, the body shook with mocking laughter and then, suddenly lifting off the ground, flew back to the shisham tree, where it hung itself from the same branch again. Vikramaditya realized that a vetala had possessed the body. Squaring his shoulders, he climbed the tree again and cut the dead body loose. This time when the corpse fell, it lay on the ground without making a sound. Descending from the tree, Vikramaditya hefted the limp form on his shoulder and began walking towards the bargad tree.

He had gone only a short distance, when the vetala in the body started speaking: 'O Raja, the wise say that those who are clever and educated spend their days in song and scripture, but the ignorant only gossip and sleep. You seem to be a wise man. Let me shorten your journey by telling you a story. Listen!'

Tale One

Who Killed Padmavati's Parents?

There is a city called Varanasi, where Lord Shiva resides. Because good people live there and the sacred Ganga surrounds it like a protector, it exudes the purity of Kailasha that is the abode of Shiva and Parvati. In the olden days, a king called Pratapamukuta ruled Varanasi. He had a son called Vajramukuta, who shattered the pride of Kamadeva with his handsome looks and the arrogance of enemies with his prowess in war. The prince had a friend, a minister's son, who loved him more than his own life. He was aptly named Buddhisharira, because he had a very sharp intellect.

One day, the two friends went hunting and, in pursuit of long-maned lions, they got separated from the royal retinue. Riding through the forest that was shrill with the sounds of birds and thick with foliaged trees, they suddenly came upon a lake. And what a lake it was—picturesque and idyllic. Its sides were lined with canopied bargad trees, sieving sunlight through their branches, while soft breezes, cool and fragrant and filled with bird song, rustled through the leaves. Sun's rays dappled its blue waters, making the many-hued lotuses glow. Bees buzzed over fragrant clusters of flowers. And hamsa birds, peacocks, and herons merrily frolicked on the banks. At a little distance from the lake was a small hillock on which stood an ancient Shiva temple.

Dismounting, the two friends led their horses to the lake and then squatted near the water's edge to splash their faces. Once they were rested, they went to the temple to bow to

Shiva. By the time they returned to the lake, a group of women had arrived there. Some of them were setting up a picnic on the bank and others were already sporting in the water. They were all beautiful, but one of them was especially so. Her animated eyes created a new forest of water lilies and the moon-lustre of her face disdained the lotuses. Her beauty was so pervasive that it filled the lake and the surroundings, and it was so captivating that it instantly captured the prince's heart.

When this woman saw a handsome young man standing by the lake, passing her slanting glances filled with longing, she, too, was enamoured. Setting aside all modesty, she told him everything about herself in a series of playful gestures: taking a water lily from her garland, she slipped it behind her ear. Then, with her ear ornament, called 'tooth-leaf', she scratched her teeth. Finally, she put a lotus against her forehead and placed one hand on her heart.

Vajramukuta did not comprehend any of the woman's gestures, and he returned home feeling as wretched as a vidyadhara who has lost all his knowledge and skills. Without saying a word to anybody he went to his room and lay down on his bed. All day, he did not eat, drink, or talk to anyone. When his attendants knocked at his door, he refused to answer, but they could hear him sigh and groan, as though he was in pain. In the evening, when Buddhisharira came to visit him and saw him in this condition, he understood immediately what ailed him. 'My friend, anyone who sets off on the path of love should give up all hope of survival, and if, by chance, he does survive, it's only to bear extreme pain and sorrow. That's why the wise never lay foot on this path.'

'It's too late for your advice. I started on this path as soon as I saw her at the lake. I just don't know how to take the next step.'

'Why don't we go and see the girl?' Buddhisharira suggested.

'How is that possible?' the prince asked. 'We don't know her name, her family, her land. How can we find her?'

'But she told you everything. Didn't you understand what she was saying?'

'What are you talking about?'

'Words are not the only way people communicate. Sometimes what is unspoken can be discerned by a person's gait or gesture, or by the expressions of the face and in the eyes. The girl we saw spoke to you in gestures.'

'What gestures?'

'Didn't you see her put a lily (utapala) behind her ear (karna)? That means that she lives in the land of Karnotapala. Then she rubbed her ear ornament on her teeth to tell you that she is the daughter of a dental physician. She also placed a lotus on her head, indicating that she is like a lotus—a padma; hence her name is Padmavati, and by placing her hand on her breast, she told you that her heart is yours.'

The prince was ecstatic to learn all this about the woman he desired. 'Thank you,' he said to his friend. 'But to find the land of Karnotapala and then to find her in that land—it'll not be easy.'

'I'm way ahead of you, my friend. I've already found that out. I had an idea about your state of mind, so I had my men dig up some information as soon as we returned from the lake. I can tell you that Kalingadesha has a city called Karnotapala, where a well-known dental physician, named Sangramavardhana lives, and that man has a jewel of a daughter called Padmavati, who is dearer to him than life.'

The prince embraced his friend in gratitude and immediately made plans to go to Kalingadesha. To avoid his parents' questions, he told them that he was going hunting with Buddhisharira and even gathered a small force of soldiers to take with him, as part of the ruse. But, as soon as his hunting party entered the forest, he and his friend kicked their horses and sped away, leaving the soldiers behind. After many days of travelling, they arrived in Kalingadesha and found their way to Karnotapala. Once they were in the city, they made enquiries about the residence of the dental physician and steered their horses in that direction. Coming to the physician's mansion, they looked for a way to enter it without being noticed, when they saw an old woman sitting in the courtyard of a small house right across from it. Seeing her, a plan began to form in Buddhisharira's mind. 'Come with me,' he said to Vajramukuta and led him to a stable, where they left their horses. Then, walking to the old woman's house, Buddhisharira approached her. 'We are businessmen,' he said to her. 'We just need a place to stay for a few days. Will you let us stay in your house?'

At first, the woman was reluctant, but when he showed her a bag of coins, she agreed.

The two friends got a good night's sleep in the old woman's house and, the following morning, Buddhisharira asked her if she knew a dental physician named Sangramavardhana.

'Yes, I do know him,' the old woman replied. 'He has a daughter called Padmavati and I'm her nurse. I've been taking care of her since she was a baby. Normally I spend my day in their house, which is that mansion right across the street, but yesterday I came home to collect some clothes. But it's my ill fortune that I don't have any clothes left. My son is an idler and a gambler, and he steals even my clothes to sell.'

Buddhisharira was very pleased to hear this and gave the old woman money to buy new clothes. 'Mother, you are kind, like our own mother,' he said. 'Please help us, but in secret.

Go and tell Padmavati that the prince she saw at the lake has come here, pulled by the magnet of her love. Also, let her know that this message is from him.'

Grateful for the money, the old woman agreed to help the young men and went to Padmavati's house to convey the message. But she returned shortly after, weeping.

'What happened?' Buddhisharira and Vajramukuta asked with concern.

'When I gave Padmavati your message, she first scolded me and then slapped me on both my cheeks. Her hands were smeared with a paste of camphor. Can you see the imprint of her fingers on my cheeks? I felt so insulted that I left right away and came here.'

The prince was heartbroken at Padmavati's reaction to his message, but his friend cheered him up. 'Don't be sad,' he said. 'She has sent you a message through the white imprint of her fingers on the old woman's cheeks. She's telling you to wait for ten nights of the dark fortnight after the waning moon. These are not suitable nights for a union.'

Hence, the two friends decided to spend the next ten days in the old woman's house. The minister's son sold some gold that they had brought along and with the money, he bought items of everyday need and an array of expensive food, which he had the old woman cook by bribing her with an invitation to share their meal. After ten days, they persuaded her to go back to Padmavati's house with the same message. This time when the old nurse returned, she told them, 'As I was standing quietly beside her, Padmavati herself asked me about you, and then, referring to the message you sent, she hit me on the chest with three fingers stained with her menstrual blood.'

'There's no doubt,' the minister's son said to the prince, once they were alone. 'By placing those three fingers on the old woman's heart, she is informing you that she'll be menstruating for three days, which means that you need to wait three more days.'

After three days, the prince sent the old woman back to the mansion. This time, Padmavati treated her nurse with affection. She fed her well and kept her engaged all day in different activities. In the evening, as the old woman was preparing to leave, there was a terrible uproar outside the gate. People were shouting and screaming, 'Help! This berserk elephant has broken its bounds and is trampling people.'

'You can't go through the door,' Padmavati said to her old nurse. 'The berserk elephant is loose on the road. The only way you can get home is through the garden. Climb the tree near the garden's boundary wall and, from there, grab a branch that's on the other side. Then you can get down safely and go home. I'll have my maids lower you on a roped chair from my bedroom balcony into the garden.'

When the old woman arrived at her house that evening, she described her adventurous trip to her guests.

'There you go,' said the minister's son to his friend. 'She has now demonstrated how you can get into her bedroom. You should go to her this very evening.'

Employing the same means that the old woman had used to get out of the mansion, but in reverse, Vajramukuta climbed up the tree onto the boundary wall and, from there, into the garden. Then, finding the roped chair hanging from a balcony, he sat down in it and gave the rope a tug, so that he could be pulled up.

When he stepped into Padmavati's bedroom, she was eagerly waiting for him. The two lovers fell into each other's arms, their impassioned embrace compensating for their days of separation and angst. With a quick ceremony, they performed a gandharva marriage and then spent the night in lovemaking, experimenting with each of the four positions of sexual intimacy described in the *Kamashastra*. All night they cried out and sighed, and uttered passionate sounds of pleasure until their desire was satiated. As they lay languorously in Padmavati's bed, Vajramukuta said to her, 'I'm craving a paan, dearest.'

'A paan? Not me?' Padmavati asked him with a pout.

'Don't be offended, dear lady,' he said. 'Let me tell you the thirteen virtues of an aromatic paan. It's an aphrodisiac that will increase my desire for you.'

With a flirtatious laugh, Padmavati got off the bed and brought Vajramukuta a paan, which he chewed with great relish and then tightened his arms around her again.

After that night, Vajramukuta began to stay with Padmavati, and the two of them spent all their time together, talking, laughing, playing love games, having lover's quarrels, and finding seductive ways to make up. Then, one morning, the prince said to Padmavati, 'I came here with my dear friend, Buddhisharira, who is the son of my father's minister and highly intelligent. He's staying in the house of your old nurse. But he must be lonely without me. I'll go back there tonight, just to check on him and then I'll return to you.'

'Dear prince, I'm curious. Please tell me who interpreted all my gestures—you or your friend?'

'I'll be honest with you. It wasn't me. Buddhisharira with his superior intelligence was the one who explained each of your gestures to me.'

Padmavati was silent for a moment and then she said, 'Because he's your friend, he's like a brother to me; therefore, I should welcome him properly. Go back to your friend tonight. I'll see you tomorrow.'

Vajramukuta returned to the old woman's house, via the garden and boundary-wall path, and spent the evening with his friend. When he told Buddhisharira about his conversation with Padmavati, the minister's son shook his head. 'This doesn't bode well.'

'What do you mean?' the prince asked.

'Maybe it's nothing, or maybe it's what I fear. Let's see what she does,' Buddhisharira replied.

Early the next morning, a few of Padmavati's maids arrived at the old woman's house, bearing platters of delicious food. 'Our mistress wishes to welcome you,' they said to Buddhisharira, placing the food before him. When Vajramukuta tried to take a piece from it, they stopped him. 'Padmavati is waiting for you,' they said. 'You should go to her house and eat with her. This food is only for your friend.'

Buddhisharira thanked them and told them that he would eat after his bath. When they left, he threw a morsel to a street dog. As soon as the dog ate the food, he fell down dead.

Vajramukuta was shocked. 'What happened to the dog?' he asked his friend.

'I was suspicious of this last night when you told me about the questions Padmavati was asking about me and when I saw her maids this morning, I knew her intention. She wanted to poison me. You see, she has understood that you and I are very close, and she's jealous. She doesn't want to share you with me. She's also afraid that I may persuade you to return to your kingdom. But don't be angry with her. She's only doing this out of love for you. I think you should persuade her to elope with you. Let me think of a plan.'

As the two were talking, they heard loud noises in the street outside. People were running towards the royal palace, calling, 'The king's son is dead!'

This news pleased the minister's son. 'Listen,' he said to Vajramukuta. 'Tonight, go back to Padmavati and get her drunk, to the extent that she passes out. Then, take the trishool I will give you and, firing up its prongs, mark her near the groin. After that, collect all her ornaments in a bundle and bring them to me. I'll take it from there.'

That night, carrying the small, sharp-pronged trishool, Vajramukuta returned to Padmavati's bedroom through her window. He then proceeded to get her drunk and when she passed out, he fired up the tips of the trishool on a lamp and touched it to her inner thigh, near the groin. After that, gathering all her ornaments and tying them in a bundle, he left her bedroom via the roped chair.

The following morning, Buddhisharira took Vajramukuta to the cremation ground, where he disguised himself as an ascetic and his friend as his initiate. Then he took one pearl necklace from the jewellery bundle and told his friend to try and sell it in the market. 'But put such a high price on it that no one will be able to afford it. Go all over town with the necklace; the more people that hear about it, the better,' he instructed him.

'Why should I try to sell it, if you don't want it sold?' Vajramukuta asked.

'I have a plan. When Padmavati recovers from her drunkenness, she'll inform her father that her jewellery has been stolen and he'll inform the king. The king will send out soldiers to search for the thief. These soldiers will apprehend you, because they'll have heard about your attempts to sell Padmavati's necklace. That's my goal. Don't resist arrest. When the soldiers ask you where you got the necklace from, just say that your guru gave it to you, and bring them here to me. I'll take care of the rest.'

The prince did exactly as his friend instructed, and when the soldiers caught him and asked him how he got the necklace, he took them to the cremation ground, where Buddhisharira was waiting in the guise of an ascetic. He was seated in a lotus position, his hair was piled on his head in a bun, and his eyes were half-closed, as though in deep meditation.

'O holy man,' the soldiers said to him. 'Your student has a pearl necklace that he says you gave him to sell. Where did you get that necklace from?'

'I'm an ascetic. I wander from place to place. Last night I stayed here in this cremation ground. There were also yoginis and dakinis here, and one of them was carrying the king's son. I saw her tear open the boy's chest and sacrifice his heart to Lord Bhairava. Then she became intoxicated with alcohol and, in that inebriated state, she began harassing me, demanding that I give her the holy rudraksha beads that I was counting. I tolerated her for a while, but, finally, I couldn't take it any more, so I took my trishool, heated its tips with the fire of my mental power, and pierced that dakini's groin. She ran away. But before she left, I was able to grab this necklace that was around her neck. I'm an ascetic. I have no use for ornaments, such as this necklace; that's why I wanted to sell it.'

The soldiers went to the king and related the whole story to him. What the king concluded from this account was that his son was killed by a dakini, who was wearing a pearl necklace that belonged to the dental physician's daughter. This dakini could be easily identified by the burn mark she bore from the ascetic's trishool. Therefore, the woman who had this mark and owned the necklace was his son's killer. Since Padmavati was the owner of the necklace, the king sent an old, trusted woman to find out if she also had a trishool-burn mark on her groin. When the old woman confirmed it, the king closed the case; he had no doubt that Padmavati was the culprit. 'But how should I punish this dakini?' he asked himself. 'She's a woman, but not like any other. She's a being born from nature and exists in nature. But she has committed a grave crime against a human and must be punished for it.' Then he thought he should get advice from the ascetic in the cremation ground who seemed to know about yoginis and dakinis. Hence, the king went to the ascetic and asked him how he should punish the dakini.

'Brahmins and cows should not be killed,' said the ascetic. 'Neither should women and children or kinsmen, or those with whom one has shared a meal. And those who seek sanctuary are to be always protected. For women of all kinds, who commit a crime, the harshest punishment should be banishment. Therefore, O King, my advice is—exile that dakini from your city.'

Thus, the king ordered his men to take Padmavati to the forest outside the city and leave her there.

That evening, discarding their disguises, the prince and his friend rode to the forest, where the king's soldiers had deposited the exiled Padmavati, and persuaded her to come with them to Varanasi. Finally, Prince Vajramukuta and his beloved Padmavati were able to be together without having to keep their relationship secret. It is true that if something is truly hidden, even Brahma can't know it. But if a person is trying to discover the truth, it behoves him to thoroughly investigate before jumping to conclusions; otherwise, he will regret it.

Padmavati's parents did not know about their daughter's secret affair, and they had no idea about her escape to Varanasi. When they were told that the king's men had left her in the forest, they tried to look for her there, and when they did not find her, they thought she had been devoured by wild beasts. Grieving for her, Padmavati's father passed away and her mother gave herself up to his pyre.

'King, you are a very wise man,' said the vetala from the corpse on Raja Vikramaditya's shoulder. 'Let me ask you a question. Who do you think incurred the sin of killing Padmavati's parents: Buddhisharira, the minister's son; Vajramukuta, the prince; or Padmavati herself? If you know the answer, you must speak it, because if you don't, your head will shatter into a thousand pieces.'

'The matter is clear,' Vikramaditya replied. 'The sinner is the king of Karnotapala.'

'How is he the sinner? He hardly played any part in all that happened. It was the other three who were carrying on the affair.'

'Those three can't be blamed. Whatever the minister's son did was for his prince's well-being. The other two—the prince and Padmavati—they were burning in the fire of desire and not thinking clearly. They can't be held responsible for their actions. On the other hand, Raja Karnotapala was not only an objective observer, but he was also a king. Being a king, he knew the laws of justice and should have followed them. Yet, he made no enquiries about anyone—neither about the ascetic and his initiate, nor about Padmavati. And he gave a verdict without any thought or deliberation, or even rationale. Therefore, the entire sin of the death of Padmavati's old parents is his.'

At Vikramaditya's response, the dead body that was hanging on his shoulder, suddenly straightened like an arrow and flew to the shisham tree, where it hung itself from a branch again.

Tale Two

Who Deserves Mandaravati?

Raja Vikramaditya walked back to the shisham tree and climbed it again. Reaching the corpse, he cut it loose and let it drop to the ground. When it fell, it again cried out, as though it was in excruciating pain, but this time, the king paid it no heed. Jumping down, he lifted the body on his shoulder and began walking in the direction of the bargad tree.

'What a situation you've put yourself in, O Raja,' said the vetala inhabiting the corpse. 'This must be so stressful for you. Let me tell you another story to alleviate your stress.'

On the bank of river Yamuna is a village called Brahmasthala. Once, a Vedic brahmin by the name of Agniswami lived there. He had a daughter, Mandaravati, whose beauty was so flawless that after crafting her, the creator must have looked disparagingly at his own heavenly apsaras, who are considered the epitome of beauty.

By the time Mandaravati reached her youth, her exquisite beauty had already made her a legend. Agniswami received numerous marriage proposals for her, but none of them met the criteria of a groom that he had in mind for his daughter. Then, three handsome young men, who were replete with every quality he desired, came from the country of Kanyakubja to press their suit. They were equally handsome and equally suited. Agniswami was in a dilemma. He liked all three of them and did not know whom to pick. Therefore, he invited the three suitors to stay in his house for a few days so that he could learn more about them from their day-to-day behaviours. However, Agniswami found no opportunity to observe their qualities, because all they did, all day long, was gaze at Mandaravati's moonlike face, like love-sick chakor birds.

Then, as fate would have it, Mandaravati was bitten by a black snake and she became very sick with a high fever, extreme nausea, and debilitating paralysis. Agniswami tried everything he could to save her, summoning physicians from lands far and near, hiring snake venom extractors, and performing fire sacrifices with mantra-chanting brahmins; but no one could save Mandaravati. It is said that if someone gets bitten by a venomous black snake on the fifth–sixth, eighth–ninth, or the fourteenth day of the waning moon, the bite is fatal, and so it proved to be for Mandaravati, too, who was bitten on the ninth day.

Agniswami was devastated by his daughter's death, but even more shattered than him were the three young suitors from Kanyakubja. They accompanied Mandaravati's flower-shrouded body to the bank of the river Yamuna and wailed loudly at the injustice when she was prepared for cremation. When her pyre was lit, one of the young men jumped into the flames and killed himself, hoping to unite with her in the afterlife. Another suitor built a small, rough-hewn hut of mud and wood over Mandaravati's cremation site and began living there like a bhikshu, hoping to always be connected to the place where her body had last touched the earth. The third suitor chose a different path. To seek release from the pain of Mandaravati's memories and passing, he became a wandering sadhu, going from place to place, begging for his food, and listening to holy men talk about the transience of life.

One day, this wanderer arrived in the village of Vajraloka. As he was begging for his food, a brahmin invited him into his house for a meal. Accepting the invitation, he followed the host into the kitchen, where his wife was cooking, and sat down on a mat. Seated beside the brahmin's wife was their young child, who was crying incessantly. The mother cajoled the child several times and then scolded him, but the boy just kept on crying. Finally, frustrated at his behaviour, the brahmin's wife picked him up and threw him into the kitchen fire. In no time the flames consumed his tender flesh and burnt him to ashes. The wanderer from Kanyakubja was horrified. Jumping up, he began shouting at the brahmin, 'Is this a house of a rakshasa? How could your wife throw her own child into the flames? Such ruthlessness is evil. I'll not eat a single grain in this house. It's a house of sinners.' And, leaving the kitchen, he rushed to the front door.

'Wait, O Sadhu,' the brahmin called after him. 'What you saw is not what it looks like. I've obtained a power. Please come and watch what this power can do.'

The wandering man reluctantly followed the brahmin back into the kitchen and took a seat, while the brahmin went into another room and returned with a book. Sitting down, he opened the book on his lap and read a mantra from it. Then, he took water in a cupped palm and sprinkled it on the ashes of the child. Before an eye could even blink, the little boy rose out of the fire and stood beside his mother, with not a burn mark on him.

The wanderer was amazed and his immediate thought was, can this mantra revive my beloved Mandaravati? Therefore, he decided to steal the book. Requesting the brahmin to let him stay the night, he watched him put the book in a bag and hang it from a nail on a wall. When the brahmin and his wife fell asleep, he quietly took the book bag and crept out of the house.

After travelling for many days and nights, the wanderer arrived at the site where Mandaravati had been cremated and the second suitor had built his hut. 'Come out,' he called to that man. 'We need to break down your hut.'

The other man came out, looking confused. 'Why do you want to break down my sanctuary?' he asked. 'I feel close to my beloved Mandaravati here.'

'But what if I bring her back to life?'

'What do you mean?' the other man asked, and the wanderer told him about the scene he had witnessed in the brahmin's house and showed him the mantra book.

The two of them together quickly pulled down the hut. Then the wanderer opened the book, read the mantra, and sprinkled water on the cremation site. To their utmost delight, Mandaravati, instantly, stood before them in full loveliness, as though she had never been sick from the snake bite and had never burned to ashes. As the two young men stood gazing upon their beloved, the third man, who had jumped into the fire and perished along with her, also came back to life.

At first, the three young men rejoiced at seeing each other. But then they began to quarrel about who deserved to be Mandaravati's husband. Their quarrel grew into a brawl and soon they were exchanging kicks and blows and putting each other in headlocks.

'I ask you, O King,' said the vetala to Raja Vikramaditya, 'Who do you think deserves Mandaravati—the man who brought her back to life with the mantra, the one who immolated himself on her pyre and died with her, or the one who lived on her cremation site to always remain connected with her? Be warned that if you know the answer and don't speak it, your head will shatter into a thousand pieces.'

'The one who read the mantra was like her father, because he gave her life. How can he be her husband? The one who killed himself and was born again with her is like her brother. How can he be her husband? He who chose to live next to her cremation site so that he could think about her day and night is the only one who behaved like her husband. Therefore, it is he who deserves to marry her.'

As soon as Vikramaditya gave the answer, the corpse flew off his shoulder and went and hung itself from the same branch of the shisham tree. But the king was determined to keep his word to Kshantisheela; hence, he turned around and retraced his steps.

Tale Three

Are Men More Deceiving Than Women?

Cutting the corpse loose again, Raja Vikramaditya jumped down from the shisham tree and threw the dead body over his shoulder. When he began walking in the direction of the bargad, the vetala spoke to him again: 'O Raja, you're labouring so hard in the middle of the night. Let me divert your mind with an amusing tale.'

In this world is the very famous city of Pataliputra. In the olden days, it used to be ruled by a king called Rupasena, whose brilliance shone like a priceless gem. This king had a pet parrot, whose name was Vidagdachuramani, and he was an erudite scholar of metaphysics, astrology, and astronomy. This parrot had been a savant in his past life and was cursed to be born as a parrot, but he was allowed to retain his full memory and scholarship.

The king treated his parrot like a friend, advisor, and confidante. Therefore, when he began to contemplate matrimony, he asked his parrot for advice: 'In this world, is there a woman who is a perfect match for me?'

'There is, Maharaj,' the parrot replied. 'The beautiful Princess Chandraprabha of Magadha is your perfect match.'

Princess Chandraprabha of Magadha was, indeed, comely and talented. She also had a pet myna called Madanamanjari, who was the embodiment of love and its exuberance, as her name—blast of love's blossoms—suggested. Just when Raja

Rupasena was talking to his parrot about suitable brides, Chandraprabha was also asking her myna the same question: 'In this world, is there a man who is the perfect match for me?'

'There is, Rajkumari,' the myna replied. 'The king of Pataliputra. His name is Rupasena—a name that truly describes him. His face is the most handsome in the world and he has a personality that is most charming.'

The myna's description of Rupasena struck Chandraprabha like Kamadeva's arrows, and she began to pine for him. Fortuitously, soon after, an embassy from Pataliputra arrived in Magadha with Raja Rupasena's marriage proposal for Rajkumari Chandraprabha. The proposal was accepted, and, in due time, amidst great rejoicing by the populace of both kingdoms, Rupasena and Chandraprabha were married in an elaborate Vedic ceremony.

After the nuptials, Raja Rupasena introduced his parrot, Vidagdachuramani, to Chandraprabha's myna, Madanamanjari, and gently placed her in the parrot's cage. Vidagdachuramani was immediately smitten by the myna, and he began to woo her. One day, he said to her, 'We live together in the same cage, we eat together from the same dish, we sit on the same perch, and we see each other all the time. Why don't you join me in my bed as well? We're young and life is fleeting. The wise say that every being experiences carnal pleasure, and it's also said that young and innocent ladies should learn such pleasures from an experienced lover. Only a few males know the secrets of Kamadeva and I'm one of them. Let me show you love's enjoyment; it's a state of being that brings one ecstasy equal to heaven.'

'Get away from me,' the myna cried. 'I don't want anything to do with you or any other male. Males are wicked, inconsiderate, and ungrateful. They cause us females much pain.'

'Men are not the wicked ones; it's the females who are wicked,' retorted the parrot. 'They lie and cheat and destroy males. The hearts of females are made of stone.'

'And the hearts of males are made of quicksilver, never steady, attracted to one female at one moment and to another in the next moment.'

'And females? They only know how to deceive.'

Exchanging such insults, the parrot and the myna got into such an argument about who was more wicked that they needed the king's intervention.

'Why do you say that males are wicked, inconsiderate, and ungrateful?' Raja Rupasena asked the myna.

'Let me tell you a story, Maharaj,' the myna replied. 'That will amply prove to you the truth of what I say.'

'Kamandaki is a renowned city. Once, a very wealthy businessman called Arthadatta lived there with his son, Dhanadatta. From the moment the boy was born, his parents fulfilled his every wish and never refused him anything. Therefore, the boy grew up unruly and spoilt. To make matters worse, when he entered his youth, he began to keep company with a bad lot who introduced him to gambling. Soon, Dhanadatta was so addicted to games of chance that he hardly ever left the gambling dens. For many years, he squandered his father's wealth, and then Arthadatta passed away. Now, Dhanadatta, who had never learned how to manage his father's business, began to depend on his friends to guide him about matters of money. Needless to say, before long, Dhanadatta lost the entirety of his father's wealth and became destitute. The wise rightly say that the tree of bad times has roots in bad company.

Reduced to penury and embarrassed by his situation, Dhanadatta left Kamandaki to go to another city where no one would know him. As he was travelling through the town of Chandanapura, hunger pangs forced him to stop, and he knocked at the door of an affluent-looking house, hoping to get some food. It was the residence of a rich moneylender, who not only invited Dhanadatta in for a meal but also treated him like an honoured guest. He was given cool water to wash himself and fresh clothes to change into. After that, he was seated on a comfortable mat and served a meal on a silver platter laden with all sorts of delicacies. As Dhanadatta ate, the moneylender sat across from him, chatting with him and keeping him company. In the course of the conversation, he asked him who he was, who his father was, where he was headed, and why he was making the journey.

Dhanadatta answered him, but with half-truths that did not reveal his impoverished state. "My name is Dhanadatta," he said. "As for my father—his name was Arthadatta, and he was a very wealthy businessman. At his death, he left me all his wealth. Before I settle down, I want to travel to different places; that is the purpose of my journey. I don't have a destination yet, because I'm still trying to decide where to settle down."

The moneylender was very pleased with Dhanadatta's answers. Impressed by his handsome looks and pleasant demeanour, he had already been considering him as a possible husband for his daughter and, after he learned that he came from a wealthy, business family, he was convinced of the suitability of the match. "I want to thank you for gracing my home, son," he said to Dhanadatta. "I have a proposition for you. Since you don't have a fixed destination, why don't you stay here in my house as my son-in-law? My daughter is of age, and I've been thinking about finding her a suitable husband. But it seems that her destiny has preempted me and has, itself, brought her intended groom to my house. Her name is

Ratnavati, and, true to her name, she shines like a gem. She's also gentle and caring and imbued with all good qualities."

Dhanadatta accepted the proposal, and, within a few days, he and Ratnavati were married. After the nuptials, Dhanadatta began to live in his father-in-law's house. For a while, married life stemmed his addiction to gambling, and he behaved with his wife and her family as a good son-in-law and husband should. However, before long, feeling a familiar itch, he told his father-in-law that he needed to return to his own land.

"Son, I'm getting old, and you and Ratnavati are my only support. I beg you to stay. If it's a business matter, go and take care of it. But then come back and don't talk about leaving me again."

"I have to go," Dhanadatta insisted. "Please give me permission to leave and to take my wife with me."

The old father-in-law had no choice but to give his blessing. He performed the appropriate rites of a daughter's departure and, with tears flowing down his wrinkled cheeks, bade her farewell. Bedecked in expensive jewellery and accompanied by an old maid, Ratnavati started on the journey with her husband.

After many hours of walking, they came to the foot of a steep hill. "Wife, our path lies on the other side of this hill," Dhanadatta said to Ratnavati. "We must climb it to go across."

"Alright," said Ratnavati and began to trudge up the hill, along with her maid. On the top of the hill was a forest.

"Dear wife, we have to cross this forest," Dhanadatta said. "But there are always thieves and robbers lurking in it. The jewellery you're wearing will attract their attention. Why don't you remove all your jewels and your fine silk shawl and let me carry them concealed under my shirt? Once we're out of the forest, I'll give them back to you."

Thanking her fate for giving her such a caring and

considerate husband, Ratnavati unwrapped her expensive silk shawl and removed all the gold and jewels she was wearing. Tying them in the shawl, she handed the bundle to Dhanadatta. He took it and slipped it under his shirt. Then, stepping closer to her, he suddenly pushed her with both his hands. Ratnavati stumbled and tried to grab him in confusion, but Dhanadatta kept pushing her till she reached the edge of the hill and tumbled over. After that, he turned to her old maid and, with one big shove, sent her hurtling down the hill as well. Then, without a second look, he ran into the forest and disappeared. In that moment, he was a wicked man, whose heart had become as cold and cutting as a sword.

Ratnavati's old maid died before her body hit the ground, but Ratnavati, somehow, managed to grab on to a bush as she fell. She hung there, screaming for help, until her fingers grew numb. However, her lifespan was not over yet. A passerby heard her cries for help and, quickly making a rope of his turban, pulled her up to safety. For a while, Ratnavati lay on the hill, crying piteously and bemoaning her fate. Then she wiped her tears, got on her feet, and began to look for a way home.

When her father saw his daughter at his door, with her face and arms bleeding and her eyes red-rimmed and swollen, he was beside himself with concern. "What has happened?" he cried. "Why have you come back, and why are you in this state? And where is your husband?"

"Father, we were attacked by robbers," she told him. She didn't have the heart to tell her old father that he had been deceived and had married his only daughter to a man who was a robber himself. "They forcibly took my husband," she explained further. "I don't know whether he's alive or dead. And they pushed me and amma down a cliff. Amma died, but I managed to hold on to a bush, and by the grace of the gods, a stranger heard my cries for help. He pulled me up and saved me."

"Oh, my dear daughter," the old man cried, gathering her in his arms. "I thank the gods that you're alive, and I hope my son-in-law escapes those evil men. In the meantime, stay here, safely, in your father's house."

Back in his city, Dhanadatta sold his wife's jewellery and shawl and met up with his old friends again. And, in no time at all, he lost all the money in gambling. When not a paisa remained, he began to think of his father-in-law. "I should go back to Chandanapura and visit him," he said to himself. "I'll tell him that I was in the area on business and stopped by to pay him a visit. And if he asks about his daughter, I'll tell him that she's living happily with me in my house in Kamandaki. I'll stay for a few days and enjoy the comfort of his house, and when I leave, he'll surely give me many expensive gifts and, perhaps, even bags of money. After all, I'm his son-in-law."

Confident that his plan would work, he arrived in Chandanapura and headed towards the moneylender's house. As he was coming down the street, Ratnavati saw him from a window. She rushed out to meet him and, falling at his feet, told him about the story she had made up for her father. "I couldn't tell my old father the truth," she cried. "I beg you to please keep my secret."

Dhanadatta was shocked to see his wife still alive, and he agreed to do as she asked.

The moneylender was overjoyed to see his son-in-law, and he celebrated the occasion by inviting his friends and acquaintances to a lavish feast. On the day of the feast, Dhanadatta couldn't help but notice the fine jewels his wife was wearing. Salivating at the thought of getting his hands on them, his heart became the epitome of evil. That night, when

Ratnavati came into their room, Dhanadatta grabbed her and strangled her and, taking all her jewellery, ran away.

'So you see, Maharaj, how that evil man took advantage of the trust that Ratnavati and her old father put in him? This is the nature of men. One can never trust them. They are always thinking of their own gain, even if it means cheating and deceiving others, or even killing them.'

'I hear what you are saying,' said the king. 'Now let me hear what the parrot has to say.'

'Maharaj, women are the evil ones,' the parrot declared. 'They are unethical, inconsiderate, and without shame. Let me tell you a story to prove this.'

'There is a city called Harshavati. A millionaire businessman, called Dharmadatta, used to live there with his wife and daughter. The daughter's name was Vasudatta, and she was exquisitely beautiful and dearer to Dharmadatta than his own life. When she came of age, he married her to a young man called Samudradatta. He was from the town of Tamralipta, and his family was equally wealthy and well established in business. Not only that, he was also a very attractive man, with a moon-like face that is the quintessence of love's desire.

Some weeks after the wedding, Samudradatta had to go out of town for business, and Vasudatta went to stay with her father till he returned. In her husband's absence, Vasudatta lost all sense of what is right and what is wrong. One day, when she was standing on the terrace with her friend, the garland-maker's daughter, Vasudatta saw an extremely handsome young man pass by in the street below. She was instantly struck with desire. It's true what they say: a woman is like a jar of butter and a man, especially one who is well groomed and handsome, is a flaming fire. When the two come together, the butter melts. But a married woman must curb herself and be faithful to her husband. That is what the shastras say. But Vasudatta gave no thought to the shastras or her husband and said to her friend, "Go quickly and stop that man. Tell him I want to meet him. I'm burning with desire for him."

The garland-maker's daughter ran into the street and, catching up with the young man, told him that her friend had seen him from the terrace and fallen in love with him. Then she set up a meeting for them in her own house. From then on, Vasudatta and the young man became lovers, and they began to meet regularly.

Some months later, Vasudatta's husband returned from his business travels and went to fetch her from her father's house. Dharmadatta and his wife were very pleased to see their son-in-law and hosted a feast in his honour. After the feast, Vasudatta's mother cajoled her into dressing as a new bride again to welcome her husband home. With reluctance, Vasudatta put on bridal clothes and went to her husband's room. Samudradatta was delighted to see his wife, and he was especially happy to see her dressed as a bride. "I've missed you, beloved," he said, embracing her and drawing her down on the bed. "I've waited a long time to be reunited with you."

Vasudatta gave him a wan smile and tried to pull out of his embrace, but he tightened his arms around her, whispering in her ear how much he loved and desired her. Far from responding to his impassioned words, Vasudatta's body stiffened. She now thrilled only at her lover's touch. Breaking free from Samudradatta's embrace, she snapped at him, "I'm tired from the feast," and turning on her side, lay down with her back to him.

When a woman is excited to be with her lover, her face, her expressions, her words, her gaze, her gestures—everything gives her away. But when she rejects him, just one instance of knitted brows, one cold word, or one single act of turning away can amply convey her feelings.

Samudradatta was disappointed, but being weary from the journey and inebriated, he soon fell asleep. When a man is filled with passion, sleep is the farthest thing on his mind, even if the bedsheets are silk and the bed itself is a haven of comfort. But when a man is freed of passion, he can sleep even on a hard rock or a bed of thorns.

Vasudatta waited for her husband to fall asleep. Then, slipping out of the room, she quietly left the house. As she hurried to the main gate, a thief who had just jumped over the wall saw her. He quickly hid behind a bush to watch her. In the moonlight, he could see her fine silk clothes and glittering ornaments. Who is this woman decked in jewellery and clothes that are every thief's dream, and where is she going, he wondered. Is she a wanton woman who has left her husband's side and is off to see one of her many lovers? Or is she a deserted woman, who has been awaiting word from her stalling lover and has decided to go to him and gauge his intention? Or maybe she's a bold woman, who is impatient to feel her lover's embrace and to drink the nectar of his sweet lips; that's why she has dispensed with messengers and is going herself to commit to her love. Then, another thought came to him: instead of stumbling about in the dark house and putting myself in jeopardy, why don't I just follow this woman and rob her? And so the robber began to follow Vasudatta as she stepped out of the main gate and started walking in the direction of the park, where she had an assignment with her lover that night.

However, what Vasudatta found in the park was not her eager lover waiting for her with open arms but his dead body hanging from a tree with a noose around the neck. "Oh, what cruelty is this?" she cried and sank to the ground, sobbing.

"Did you know this man?" Two security guards, who were standing near the hanging man, asked Vasudatta.

"Yes," she nodded. "I knew him."

"We saw him lurking here and asked him several times who he was and what he was up to, but he refused to tell us. There have been many robberies in this neighbourhood and he looked very suspicious."

"He was not a robber," she cried.

"Our apologies. We were just following the king's orders," they said. Then one of them cut the body loose and laid it on the ground.

Once the security guards had left, Vasudatta got up and gathered flowers to spread on her lover's lifeless body. Then she sat down beside him and took his head in her lap. "Oh, my dearest, I'll miss our secret meetings and lovemaking so much." She sobbed and kissed his cold lips.

The thief, who had followed Vasudatta to the park, watched her from a distance, debating whether he should still do what he had come to do and snatch her jewellery. What irony of fate is this, he thought: she expected to be in the warm embrace of her lover but now holds his cold body in her embrace. And I expected to warm my pockets with her jewels, but now I'm standing here watching the cold glitter of them around her neck.

Aside from the robber, someone else was also watching Vasudatta. It was a mischievous yaksha, who was thinking, what if I enter the body of the lover and make him come alive? That way the woman can have one last lovemaking with her lover and I can enjoy her body. The next instance, he slipped into the body of the dead lover.

Feeling the corpse in her arms begin to stir, Vasudatta cried out in shock. Then, all of a sudden, her lover's arms were around her, holding her tightly, and her body was already getting aroused. Soon, she was experiencing a sexual intensity she had never before felt. When she was in the last throes of it, the yaksha suddenly left the corpse, but, before he vanished, he playfully bit off Vasudatta's nose.

In the midst of pleasure, Vasudatta screamed in pain and let go of her lover's body that had gone limp again. Getting up hurriedly, she ran out of the park, with blood pouring down her face, and went to her friend's house. When her friend answered the door, she fell into her arms and sobbed out the events of the night. Her friend was very sympathetic. "I don't know if your lover came back to life or some evil spirit entered his body," she said. "What I do know is that your nose has been cut off. How will you explain that to your husband and parents?"

"What should I do? What should I say?" she cried. "Help me!"

The friend came up with a plan: "Quickly return to your house," she said, "and get into bed with your husband, but make sure you don't wake him. Then, start crying loudly and call out to your parents. When they come, tell them your husband has done this to you."

Vasudatta did exactly as her friend advised. She ran to her house and slipped into her room. Her husband was still sleeping soundly. Tiptoeing to the bed, she quietly got in and let out a loud shriek, followed by wailing and calls for help.

Everyone in the house was jostled out of sleep, and they ran to Vasudatta's room to see what the matter was. There, they saw Vasudatta sitting in bed with a bloodied face and a bitten off nose and Samudradatta rubbing his eyes, looking very confused.

"Father," Vasudatta cried, "he has bitten off my nose and disfigured me."

"Why have you done this to my daughter?" Vasudatta's father shouted at Samudradatta.

Samudradatta turned to look at his wife and was stunned at what he saw. "What are you saying?" he said to her. "I didn't do that to you."

"Are you saying I'm lying?" she accused. "Who else could have done it? There's no one here but you. You're the one who did it."

Samudradatta was rendered speechless. He thought, it is better to trust a black serpent or an enemy with a sword, or even a man who is crazy, but a woman should never be trusted. Who can understand why wild horses stampede, or clouds suddenly burst in spring, or rain fails to come when it's expected, or a woman acts the way she does?

"You wicked man. How dare you do this to my daughter?" Vasudatta's father advanced threateningly towards Samudradatta, but the other relatives grabbed his arms and stopped him. "This is a matter for the magistrate," they advised. "Let Vasudatta seek justice in the king's court."

In the court, standing before the magistrate, Samudradatta repeatedly swore that he was innocent, but no one believed him.

"You have disfigured your beautiful, innocent wife," the magistrate declared. "This is a serious crime and for this you will be hanged."

Then a voice from the back of the courtroom said, "Respected Nyayadhisha, please wait." It was the thief. He had followed Vasudatta from the park to her friend's house, and from there to her own residence and, finally, to the court. Hence, he had witnessed every act of this drama. "This man is innocent," he declared.

"Who are you and what proof do you have?" the magistrate asked the thief. "Come forward and state what you know about this case."

The thief stepped forward and narrated the night's affairs.

For proof, he told the magistrate where the lover's corpse was lying. "If you look inside his mouth, you'll probably find this woman's nose there," he said.

Sure enough, when the lover's corpse was brought into the court and his mouth opened, they found Vasudatta's nose between his teeth.

The magistrate revoked the verdict against Samudradatta and let him go free. As for Vasudatta—her ears were cut off as well. Then she was mounted on a donkey and chased out of the kingdom.

'You see, Maharaj,' said Vidagdachuramani the parrot, 'this is the true nature of women—heartless and deceiving.'

As soon as the parrot's story ended, he and the myna bird suddenly changed form: the parrot became a vidyadhara and the myna became the apsara, Tilottama. Bowing to the king, they told him that they had been under a curse that was lifted as soon as they told the stories.

Then they both ascended to Indra's heaven.

'Now, I ask you, O Raja,' said the vetala to Vikramaditya, 'who do you think is more deceiving—women or men? If you know the answer, you must speak it, or you know what'll happen to your head.'

'Men are taught to distinguish between good and evil, and they are always directed to refrain from evil. Therefore, men are less likely to commit evil acts. Women, on the other hand, are more wilful and less discerning; therefore, I would say that women are more deceiving.'

The vetala on Vikramaditya's shoulder chortled and the corpse flew right back to the shisham tree. The raja also turned around and returned to the tree.

Tale Four

Who Is the Most Noble in Viravara's Story?

'O Raja, what if I tell you that all your effort to bring me to that evil sanyasi is futile?' the vetala said to Vikramaditya as he lifted the dead body on his shoulder again and started in the direction of the bargad tree. 'Still, since you insist on continuing, I'll tell you another story to pass the time.'

There is a great city called Vardhamana. In ancient times, it used to be ruled by the meritorious Shudraka. He was the kind of king whose laws are sharp, but his punishment is gentle; who is addicted to dharma, not to women, wine, or hunting. One day, a handsome and noble kshatriya from Malwa came to Raja Shudraka, seeking employment. 'Maharaj,' he said, 'my name is Viravara and I would like to serve you. I have three means of service—a dagger tied at my waist, a sharp sword in one hand, and a shining shield in the other.'

'What wages do you want?' the king asked.

'A thousand gold coins every day,' Viravara replied.

'How many soldiers, elephants, and horses do you have to maintain?' the king asked.

'None, Maharaj. It's just me and my family—my wife, Dharmavati; my daughter, Viravati; and my young son, Sattavara.'

The king was surprised at how highly Viravara valued his services, but he was very impressed by his confidence. He was also curious to know how an ordinary man with a small family would spend so much money every day. Therefore, Shudraka hired Viravara at the salary of a thousand gold coins a day, and he appointed spies to watch him all day and report how he spent his money and time. This is what the spies reported: out of the one thousand coins, Viravara gave two hundred to his wife for the family's expenditure; with one hundred, he purchased clothes, garlands, and other aids for his own toilet; he used another two hundred for worship at the Shiva and Vishnu temples; and the remaining he gave away to beggars and brahmins. The report also stated that Viravara patrolled the main gates of the palace every day, all day and all night, except for a brief break in the afternoon when he went home to bathe and eat. After that, he returned to his post and stayed there for the remainder of the day and through the night. Because the details of the report remained unchanged day after day, Shudraka called off the watch.

A few weeks after Viravara started working for Raja Shudraka, the monsoon arrived, and rain began to pelt Vardhamana day and night. On some days, it was so heavy that it battered down like pestles. Curious to know how Viravara managed to patrol the gates in such weather, Shudraka began to check on him. Every time he passed by his bedroom window, he would glance down at the palace gate to see if Viravara was still there, and, sure enough, he would see the brave man at the lion gate, standing like an immobile pillar. One day, when the sheets of rain were so thick that it was difficult to see beyond an arm's length, Shudraka came to the window and looked down, certain that Viravara would have left the gate to seek shelter. 'Who is there, watching the gate?' he called loudly. Immediately, Viravara's voice came cutting through the rain like a well-honed knife. 'I, Viravara, am present here.'

Shudraka was very pleased to hear the response. 'What a formidable guard he is,' he said to himself. 'It seems that nothing can deter him. He's truly devoted to his duty.'

As Shudraka was turning away from the window, his ears caught the faint sound of a woman's weeping. Concerned that one of his subjects was suffering, he called down to Viravara, 'It appears that somewhere a woman is crying. Listen.' When Viravara acknowledged that he, too, could hear the sound, the king commanded him: 'Go and find out who it is and why she is crying.'

Just at that moment, lightning flashed, and torrents of rain made the earth and sky appear as one. Shudraka suddenly felt a keen desire to see for himself how Viravara would manage his assignment in such hazardous weather; hence, on an impulse, he quickly descended the stairs and began to follow Viravara.

The sound of weeping led Viravara to a lake in the outskirts of the city. There, he saw a woman standing in the middle of the rising water. Her hair was unbound and wild around her shoulders, and around her neck was a necklace of glittering jewels. She was lamenting piteously: 'O Husband! O Merciful One! O Brave One, abandoned by you, how will I live?'

'Mother, who are you and who is your husband?' Viravara called to the woman.

'Son, I am Earth. In this present time, my husband is the pious king, Shudraka. Three days from today, he is destined to die. Knowing that I'll never again have a husband like him, I can't help but lament my loss. With my divine vision, I can see the good and bad that will occur in the aftermath of his death.'

'Mother, my ears hear your terrible words, but my heart doesn't want to accept them. You are the cause and effect of everything in this world. You must know of a way to avert this terrible tragedy,' Viravara said.

'Yes, there is a way to save his life. But it requires a great sacrifice.'

'Please tell me quickly what to do. I am willing to sacrifice everything to save my lord.'

'There's a Chandika temple near the palace. If you sacrifice your own son as an offering to the Devi, she will be pleased and grant the king a hundred years of life.'

'I'll go immediately and fetch my son. What use am I if I can't save my king?' Viravara stated.

The woman, who was Earth, vanished into the water, and Viravara started back home. Shudraka, who had heard the whole conversation, was shaken by the revelation of his imminent death, but he was also in disbelief about Viravara's willingness to sacrifice his son. Wondering what Viravara would do, he continued to follow him.

Arriving at his house, Viravara woke up his wife, Dharmavati, and told her everything. Dharmavati was the kind of wife who ensured her husband's happiness and peace—a gentle but strong wife who gave him companionship, was his confidant, and pulled his sorrow out by its roots. 'You must do whatever is necessary to save your king; it is your duty,' she said to Viravara. 'Wake up our son and tell him what you need to do so that he can prepare himself.'

Viravara then awakened his young son and told him what Earth had said. 'Our king can be saved if I sacrifice you,' he said to Sattavara. 'Son, are you willing?'

Sattavara, whose name means truth, was aptly named. He replied, 'Father, my life will serve our raja. What can be more meaningful than that? I'm blessed. We owe our very food to the raja; therefore, our life is his. Please take me to the Devi's temple and sacrifice me without hesitation.'

Viravara's heart swelled with pride on hearing these

words. 'You are truly my son,' he said and, seating him on his shoulders, began to walk to the Chandika temple, accompanied by his wife and daughter. Raja Shudraka followed them.

Inside the temple, Viravara stood Sattavara before the Devi's statue. 'Are you ready, Son?' he asked.

Sattavara nodded. Even though death hovered over his young head, he calmly bowed to the goddess and offered a last prayer: 'May the sacrifice of my life keep our Raja Shudraka alive, and may he live to be a hundred and continue to take care of the earth.'

Then, Viravara, who was standing ready with a drawn sword, raised it and sliced his son's neck. Placing the boy's severed head at Devi Chandika's feet, he prayed to her, 'May the sacrifice of my son give Raja Shudraka a hundred years of life.'

Seeing her brother's headless body, Viravati, Sattavara's sister, could not bear her sorrow. 'Oh, my brother!' she wailed, and, taking a dagger, plunged it in her heart.

With both her children dead, Viravara's wife, Dharmavati, saw no reason to continue living. Folding her hands in entreaty before her husband, she said with utmost humility, 'We have saved the king's life, but now you must give me permission to enter the flames so that I can accompany our children to the other side.'

'I understand,' Viravara replied. 'I know that without the children you won't find any happiness in this world. Therefore, I won't stop you. Wait here and I'll prepare the pyre.'

When the pyre was ready, Viravara placed the bodies of his children on it and lit it. Then his wife, with folded hands and a prayer on her lips for the king's well-being, stepped into the flames as calmly as though she were stepping into cool water.

As his family burnt to ashes, Viravara turned to the goddess and began reciting prayers filled with praise for her. When his last prayer concluded, he said to her, 'My family is gone. I have fulfilled my duty to the king. I have no more reason to live. O bestower of boons, now accept my body, which I offer to you in worship and in service for the benefit of my king, Shudraka.' And, taking his sword once again, he sliced off his own head.

Sitting in a dark corner of the temple, watching the whole family die because of him, Raja Shudraka was aghast. What unfaltering courage is this, he thought. That brave warrior and his whole family gave up their lives with utmost conviction. I've never seen or heard anything like it. How will I ever repay this? But I must, otherwise what use is this life? Feeling overwhelmed with guilt and sorrow, he pleaded with the goddess: 'O Devi, praise be to you and your benevolence. I offer you the gift of myself in exchange for the life of the valorous and noble Viravara and his virtuous family. Please accept it.' Pulling out his sword, he raised it to cut off his head.

'Don't kill yourself, Son,' Devi Chandika spoke from the statue. 'I'm pleased with your bravery and sense of compassion. Watch! I will make Viravara and his whole family alive again.'

As Shudraka stepped back into the shadows and watched, Viravara, his wife, and his two children stood up without a scratch on them. Shudraka could hardly believe his eyes, but his gratitude was immense, and tears poured down his cheeks.

Finding himself and his whole family standing before the Devi's statue, Viravara thought he had been dreaming. Did I really sacrifice my son, he wondered. Did my daughter really die? Did my wife burn herself in our children's pyre? If so, then how are they here, alive and well? Maybe this is the

Devi's grace, he reasoned, that she gave us life even after we sacrificed ourselves. Touching his forehead to the Devi's feet, he turned to his family and, gathering his children close, made his way back from the temple to his house. Then, entrusting the children to Dharmavati, he returned to the lion gate to resume his guard.

The king also made his way back to the palace, still in shock, but joyful beyond words. Reaching his bedroom, he went to the window and called down, 'Who is at the lion gate?'

'It is I, Viravara. As you had commanded, I went to see the woman who was weeping, but she may have been a yakshi or a nature spirit, because as soon as I reached there, she disappeared.'

Smiling at Viravara's response, Shudraka turned away from the window and prepared for bed. However, his mind was too overwhelmed to allow him sleep. All night he kept replaying the whole incident—how Viravara had sacrificed his son and lost his whole family, just to save his life, and how, instead of bragging about his loyalty, he had not said a word. 'Even the ocean cries out when struck by a devastating storm,' he said aloud. 'But this man's forbearance is greater. His rightfulness and sense of duty are superlative, and his generosity of spirit is unfathomable.'

The following morning, Raja Shudraka called a general assembly to which he also invited Viravara and his family. When all the citizens were present, he recounted the events of the night. Then, praising the unparalleled courage and devotion of Viravara and his family, he rewarded them with tens of villages, ten crore gold coins, and sixty times the salary that Viravara had requested.

'Now tell me, O King,' the vetala said to Raja Vikramaditya, 'who do you think is the most noble out of all these people: Viravara; his son, Sattavara; his daughter, Viravati; his wife, Dharmavati; or the king, Raja Shudraka? And don't forget that if you know the answer and remain silent, your head will shatter into a thousand pieces.'

'The answer is clear,' Vikramaditya replied. 'The most noble out of these is Raja Shudraka.'

'Why do you say that?' the vetala asked. 'Why not Viravara, the bravest of soldiers, who fulfilled his duty to the king by sacrificing his own son? Why not the son, Sattavara, who despite his young age, displayed the courage of a warrior? And why not Dharmavati, Viravara's wife, who was such an exemplary mother that she held her children to her bosom even on the pyre?'

'Viravara did what he was employed to do—to protect the king; it was his duty to serve him in whichever way he could. The son, Sattavara, was a dutiful one. He was fulfilling his duty to his father by making sure that the father fulfilled his duty to the king. And Dharmavati, the wife, fulfilled her duty as a mother, while allowing her husband to serve the king. They were all noble, but they all acted from their sense of duty to themselves and to the king. It was the king, Raja Shudraka, who didn't owe anyone anything because he was the king. Yet, he was willing to give up his life for Viravara and his family. He is the noblest of them all.'

As soon as Raja Vikramaditya gave this answer, the corpse on his shoulder shot back to the shisham tree and hung itself from a high branch.

Tale Five

Who Will Marry Somaprabha?

Once again picking up the dead body he had cut down from the shisham tree, Raja Vikramaditya threw it over his shoulder. As he started to walk towards the bargad tree, the vetala that possessed the body began to scream and screech and make all kinds of terrifying sounds to disconcert him. But Vikramaditya did not break his stride.

'O Raja, you are an obstinate man,' the vetala said. 'But I like you. Let me tell you another story.'

One of the most famous cities in the world is Ujjayini. Once, the ruler of Ujjayini was Punyasena, whose brahmin minister, Hariswami, had all the good qualities that a king desires in his high-ranking officials. Hariswami had a son, Devaswami, who, like his father, was very talented, and a daughter, Somaprabha, who was not just exceptionally beautiful but also exemplary in womanly virtues and learning. By the time Somaprabha came of age, even before her parents could begin their search for a suitable groom, word about her excellence had already spread to many regions.

One day, Somaprabha said to her parents, 'I'll only marry a man who is highly accomplished. He should be either a great warrior, a peerless scholar, a skilled artist, or a brilliant scientist; otherwise, I'll not marry at all.'

To fulfil his daughter's desire, Hariswami began to search for young men of superlative achievement, but there seemed to be a dearth of such men in Ujjayini. At this time, fortuitously, he was sent by the king as his emissary to the southern kingdom. During his visit there, the minister met a handsome young brahmin with whom he became well acquainted. One day, the young man asked him if he had a daughter.

'I do, in fact, have a daughter, and I'm searching for a suitable husband for her.'

'Would you consider me?' the young man asked.

'My daughter has stated a condition for marriage, that her husband should be either a great warrior, a scholar, an artist, or a scientist; in other words, the young man should excel in one of these professions, or she will not marry.'

The brahmin's face glowed. 'I excel in engineering,' he declared.

'Can you show me proof?' Hariswami asked him.

'I've created a flying chariot. I'll bring it tomorrow to show you.'

The next day, the young man brought a mechanical flying chariot and, inviting Hariswami to board it, flew him up to the clouds and across the sky. Hariswami was very impressed and told him that he was happy to select him as his son-in-law. 'Come to our house in Ujjayini in seven days,' he told him, 'and I'll introduce you to my daughter.'

In the meantime, in Ujjayini, a handsome young brahmin approached Devaswami and declared his suit for his sister.

'My sister has stated a condition of marriage, that she will only marry someone who is either a great warrior, or he excels in scholarship, art, or science; otherwise, she will not marry,' Devaswami informed the young man.

'There is no one better than me in archery,' the young man declared. 'I can hit an object simply by hearing its sound. No one can surpass my skill.'

'In that case, you'll be a very good match for my sister,' the brother said. 'I accept you as my brother-in-law.' The two of them then went to an astrologer to determine an auspicious date for the prospective groom and bride to meet, and learned that it was in seven days.

At about the same time, another young, good-looking brahmin approached Hariswami's wife and presented his suit for Somaprabha. Hariswami's wife, too, stated: 'My daughter will only marry a man who is either a great warrior, or a superlative scholar, or he excels in art or science.'

'I am a talented astrologer. I can trace the past through the configuration of planets, and I can predict the future. My pronouncements are never wrong.'

'I think you'll make an excellent match for my daughter,' said Somaprabha's mother and had him draw up a chart to find an auspicious day for him to visit. Learning that it was in seven days, she, too, issued the invitation for that day.

Thus, on the seventh day, all three suitors presented themselves at Hariswami's house. They were all warmly welcomed as honoured guests, but with all three expecting to marry Somaprabha, Hariswami and his wife and son were quite perplexed as to what to do. 'Dear husband,' the wife said, 'we should determine who is the most suited. All three are handsome men and excel in what they do. They all appear to be equally suitable, but how do we decide who is the best?'

'I think the engineer I selected is the best of the three,' Hariswami said. 'We should express deep regret to the other two and tell them to leave.'

'How can you say that, Father?' Devaswami exclaimed. 'Each of us selected a man because he was suitable; then how can you reject two of them outright? That would be such an insult to them. I think the best way to resolve this is to let the three of them determine who is the better man and most suited for our Somaprabha.'

Hariswami and his wife agreed to their son's suggestion and proposed this solution to the three young men. 'All three of you are excellent suitors, but only one of you can marry Somaprabha,' they stated. 'We leave it up to you to decide among yourselves who it will be.'

The three men first looked at each other, measuring the competition; then they began to argue and fling insults. Finally, when they were on the verge of coming to blows, one of them suggested, 'Why don't we leave the matter up to Somaprabha herself? Let her decide whom she wants to marry. But we all must promise that once she makes her choice, the other two will bow out, gracefully.'

'Agreed,' said the other two and requested Hariswami's wife to fetch Somaprabha.

However, Somaprabha was nowhere to be found. They searched for her everywhere—inside the house and outside in the vicinity of the house—but she seemed to have disappeared.

This is what happened to her: when Somaprabha's three suitors were bickering over who would marry her, a rakshasa, by the name of Dhumrashisva, who was also allured by the stories of Somaprabha's unparalleled beauty, entered the house, invisible to everyone, and carried her off.

Very concerned about her sudden disappearance, Somaprabha's family asked the astrologer if he could somehow locate her with the help of the stars.

'Yes, from her horoscope I can find out where she is,' the astrologer said and quickly began to calculate planetary configurations. 'She's in the Vindhya Mountains,' he declared. 'A rakshasa called Dhumrashisva has abducted her and taken her there.'

'I can fly us all to the Vindhyas in my flying chariot,' said the engineer.

'And I can shoot the rakshasa dead, just by listening to his movement,' said the archer.

Then the engineer seated everyone in his flying chariot and flew them to Vindhya Mountains. There they saw Somaprabha sitting under a tall bargad tree with a ferocious rakshasa standing guard over her. The warrior then jumped out of the chariot, hid behind a large tree, and took aim by tuning his ear to the rakshasa's heartbeat. With just one arrow, he pierced his heart and shot him dead. Somaprabha's parents ran to her and gathered her in their arms, and the engineer flew everyone back to Ujjayini.

Wearied from their misadventure, Somaprabha and her parents went to their rooms to rest, while the three suitors sat and debated who had played the most crucial role in Somaprabha's rescue. The astrologer said it was him, because he was the one who discovered where the rakshasa had taken Somaprabha. The engineer claimed he was the one, since he brought everyone to Vindhya Mountains so that Somaprabha could be rescued. The warrior said his role was the most crucial, because he killed the rakshasa.

'Do you have an answer to this, O Raja? Who do you think should marry Somaprabha?'

'The right husband for Somaprabha is obviously the warrior who shot and killed the rakshasa.'

'How so?' the vetala asked.

'The chariot-maker and the astrologer were simply helpers in accomplishing the rescue. Her true rescuer was the warrior, who resolutely drew his bow and fearlessly used his talent to shoot the rakshasa dead, just by hearing his heartbeat. It's a well-known saying that even the gods behave cautiously with a man who has the six virtues of resolve, courage, valour, strength, intelligence, and fearlessness.'

As soon as Vikramaditya said these words, the corpse on his shoulder lifted up and, shooting through the air, hung itself back on a branch of the shisham tree.

Tale Six

Who Is the Real Husband? A Case of Switched Heads

As before, Raja Vikramaditya patiently walked back to the shisham tree and climbed up to where the corpse was hanging with a rope tied around its ankles. He cut the rope with his sword and dropped the dead body to the ground. Then, jumping down, he effortlessly picked it up, threw it over his shoulder, and began walking in the direction of the bargad tree, where the tantric yogi was waiting for him.

'O Raja, you are brave and wise,' the vetala said. 'I appreciate those qualities. That's why I'll tell you another story. Listen carefully and answer my question, or you know what will happen to your head.'

In the olden days, there used to be a city called Dharmapura. Its king was Raja Dharmasheela. He was a wealthy man who wanted for nothing, but he was sonless. Once, his minister, Andhaka, said to him, 'You must know the adage, Maharaj: a sonless man's house is empty, just as a fool's heart is empty. And for a poor man, everything is empty. My advice to you is to build a Devi temple and worship the goddess every day so that she can bestow her generosity on you.'

'I hear what you're saying, Andhaka,' the raja replied. 'And I've decided to follow your advice.' He then gave orders to have a large Devi temple with a water tank constructed near the palace. When it was ready, he installed a life-size idol of the Devi in it and began to worship her every morning with sandalwood, incense, flowers, diyas, and rice grains. Hailing her as the greatest, before whom even Brahma, Vishnu, Rudra, Indra, and the other gods bowed, he proclaimed her power: 'With your strong arms you support goodness and destroy the great forces of evil, like Mahisasura, Chanda and Munda, and Raktabeeja.' He also beseeched her: 'You listen to pleas of all people on earth. I have come to you with the same hope. Please fulfil my desire.'

Touched by Dharmasheela's devotion, the Devi manifested herself in her idol and spoke to him: 'I am pleased with you. Tell me what you desire.'

'If you are pleased with me, Devi, then please bestow a son on me.'

'Granted!' said the Devi. 'You will have a heroic and majestic son.'

Raja Dharmasheela fell at the idol's feet in profuse gratitude. Ten months later, his queen gave birth to a beautiful son and Dharmasheela celebrated his birth with an elaborate charity event at the Devi temple.

The story of the Devi's manifestation and her bestowment on Raja Dharmasheela spread far and wide, and that Devi temple became famous. One day a washerman's son and his friend, travelling to Dharmapura on business, came to the Devi temple to offer worship. As they were entering the inner sanctum, they saw a stunningly beautiful young woman there. The washerman's son was instantly smitten by her. Prostrating himself before the idol, he took a silent vow: 'O Devi, if, by your grace, this woman becomes my wife, I'll offer you my head.'

After concluding their business in Dharmapura, the two friends returned home, but the washerman's son left his heart and mind behind. Consumed by thoughts of the woman he had seen at the temple, he could not eat or sleep and began to spend his days and nights lying in bed, staring at the ceiling of his room. Worried about him, his friend went to his father and advised him to send a proposal for the girl. 'He's in such a state of mind that if he doesn't soon marry her, he'll kill himself,' he warned.

The washerman immediately began to make enquiries about the girl and was glad to find out that her father was also a washerman. Without delay, he took his son to Dharmapura and began marriage negotiations with the girl's family. Soon, the two were married and the washerman's son joyfully brought his bride home, feeling utterly content with life.

Many months passed. Then, one day, the girl's father organized a celebration to which he invited all his relatives and friends, including his daughter and son-in-law and his best friend.

Arriving in Dharmapura, as the three of them were passing by the park in which the Devi temple was located, the washerman's son remembered the vow he had taken before the goddess. 'Wait here,' he said to his wife and his friend. 'I'll be right back. I just need to go into the temple to make a quick offering.' Entering the temple compound, he hurriedly took a dip in the water tank and then stepped into the sanctum sanctorum. Standing before the Devi, he took the sword that was hanging in the idol's hand and cut off his head with it.

The wife and the friend of the washerman's son waited outside the temple for some time. Then the friend decided to go in and see what was taking him so long. 'Stay right here,' he said to his friend's wife. 'I'll go and fetch him.'

When he stepped into that sanctum sanctorum and saw his friend's body and severed head lying in a pool of blood, he fell to the ground in shock. As soon as he regained his senses, he thought of his friend's wife, who was still waiting outside. 'I must go and tell her about this tragedy,' he said to himself. But then he began to think: how will I explain this to his wife, and to his family and relatives? What if they think that I murdered him to obtain his beautiful wife? No one will believe that I had nothing to do with it.

Distraught with sorrow and filled with foreboding about how the world would judge him, the friend could only see one escape. Going to the water tank, he took a dip and, returning to the sanctorum, he picked up the sword and cut off his head.

Still waiting outside the temple, the wife wondered what was keeping her husband and his friend and decided to check for herself. When she entered the sanctorum, the sight of the two headless bodies lying in rivers of blood sent her reeling, and she fainted. When she came to, she began to think: people will never believe that my husband and his friend sacrificed themselves to the Devi; they'll all blame me and, somehow, hold me responsible. In any case, what am I going to do without my husband? Thinking this, the young woman ran to the water tank to take a dip and purify herself. Then, returning to the sanctorum, she picked up the sword, closed her eyes, and raised her arm to cut off her head. However, when she tried to bring the sword down, a strong force stayed her hand. She opened her eyes to see what it was and saw the Devi standing before her. 'Daughter, ask me for a boon,' she said in a gentle voice.

'Mother, please make both my husband and his friend alive again,' the young woman pleaded.

'If that is what you want, so shall it be. Go and place their heads on their bodies, and watch.'

Trembling in awe, the young woman quickly picked up the two heads and arranged them back on the bodies. However, in her agitated state, she put the head of her husband on the body of his friend and his friend's head on her husband's body. As soon as the heads were in place, the two men came alive. They first looked at each other, then at their own bodies, and then at the woman. Then they started arguing about whose wife she was.

'What do you think, O Raja? Who is the husband of this woman?'

'The shastras actually have an answer to this question,' said Raja Vikramaditya to the vetala. 'They say, among rivers, the highest regarded is the Ganga; among mountains, it is Sumeru; and among body parts, it is the head. Therefore, he who has the head of the man whom the woman is married to is her rightful husband.'

With a cackling laugh, the dead body flew back to the tree.

Tale Seven

Who Is a Suitable Son-in-Law?

'O Raja, let me tell you another story to pass the time,' the vetala said to Vikramaditya, once he had the corpse on his shoulder again and was walking towards the bargad tree.

There is a city called Champapura, that was once ruled by Raja Champakeshwara. He and his queen, Sulochna, had a daughter, Tribhuvanasundari, whose name aptly described her, because she was, indeed, the most beautiful woman in the three worlds. Her face was like the moon, glowing and brilliant; her hair was a dark rain cloud; her eyes had the shape and innocence of a deer's; her arms were like perfectly shaped bows; her nose was sharp, like an arrow; and her cheeks were soft, like petals. Her teeth had the symmetry of pomegranate seeds; lips, the redness of peach blossoms; hands, the softness of lotuses; and complexion, the burnished look of wheat. Her waist was supple, like a tiger's, and her gait had the grace of a she-elephant. What else can be said about her, except that as she grew older, her beauty, too, increased?

When Tribhuvanasundari came of age, her parents began to worry that they would not be able to find a match for her. But when word spread to other kingdoms that the exquisiteness of Raja Champakeshwara's daughter could stun men, sanyasis, and gods alike, marriage proposals began to pour in every day. Brahmins from various kingdoms began to come to Champapura, carrying missives from their kings and princes, along with their artistically drawn portraits.

The king showed each missive and portrait to his daughter, but she rejected all of them. 'Father, it's really difficult for me to decide like this,' she said.

'Then why don't we hold a swayamvara for you, and you can see all the suitors together and make a choice?'

'I don't want a swayamvara, Father. I just want a husband who is intelligent, strong, and good-looking. Please find someone with these three qualities, and I'll accept him. This is my only condition.'

After that, Raja Champakeshwara made it known that he would only entertain those suitors for his daughter who had these three qualities. In response to that, four young men from four different lands came to Champapura and presented themselves to the king. The raja welcomed them and, once they were suitably hosted, he asked each one to explain how he had the three required virtues that the princess desired.

The first suitor said: 'My name is Panchapattika. I'm a master weaver and every day I weave five sets of fine clothing. I give one set to the temple for the gods and one set to a brahmin, the third I keep for my future wife, the fourth I sell to buy food, oil, paan, and other items of daily use, and from the sale of the fifth, I save the money. I'm sure this is ample proof of my intelligence and strength of mind. As for good looks—you can see for yourself.'

The second suitor said: 'My name is Bhashagya. I know many different languages and can even decipher the speech of birds and animals. No one can match this talent. Also, in a show of strength, I can beat the strongest. And, as for good looks—you can see for yourself.'

The third suitor said: 'I'm a king's son and my name is Khadagadhara. I'm adept at wielding weapons and my talent is unsurpassable. To learn weaponry, I trained for many years, with both body and mind and I can proudly say that there's no doubt about my intelligence. As for good looks—you can see for yourself.'

And the fourth said: 'My name is Jeevadatta. I know all the shastras. I even have the knowledge to revive the dead. I'm confident that no one can best me in my learning. The discipline it took to gain this knowledge is evidence of my strength. As for good looks—you can see for yourself.'

After hearing what all four suitors had to say, Raja Champakeshwara became very concerned. 'All four young men possess the three qualities that our daughter wants,' he said to his queen, 'therefore, all four are equally suitable. I just don't know whom to pick.'

'Why don't you describe the four of them to our daughter and let her decide?' the queen advised.

The king then went to his daughter and gave her a full account of the four young men who had come to press their suit. 'What do you think, dear daughter?' he asked after he had described each one. 'Which of the four young men would you like to marry?'

Tribhuvanasundari shyly lowered her head and remained silent.

'I ask you, King,' the vetala said to Raja Vikramaditya. 'Who do you think would be the most suitable husband for this princess?'

'The first suitor is clearly a shudra, since he's a weaver; hence, he's not suitable for the princess, who belongs to a kshatriya family. The same is true for the second, who is a vaishya, for whom knowing different languages is beneficial in business. The fourth is a brahmin, whose livelihood depends on knowing the shastras. Besides, his ability to revive the dead is unworthy of his caste. That makes him even more unsuitable. However, the third young man is clearly a kshatriya, because he's a king's son and adept at wielding the sword; therefore, a marriage alliance between him and the princess is the best.'

As soon as the vetala heard this answer, the corpse flew back to the shisham tree and hung itself from a branch.

Tale Eight

Who Is More Praiseworthy—the Raja or the Rajput?

Cutting the corpse loose and lowering it to the ground, Raja Vikramaditya jumped off the tree. Throwing the body over his shoulder again, he began to make his way to the tantric sitting under the bargad tree.

'O Raja, why have you left the comfort of your palace to wander in this dreadful place frequented by bhutas and pretas?' the vetala that possessed the body spoke again. 'Your eyes must be burning from the smoke of the pyres. To take your mind off this misery, I'll tell you another story.'

There is a great city called Mithilavati, which used to be ruled by Raja Gunadhipa. Once, a brave Rajput called Chiramadeva came from a faraway land with the intention of serving the king. He went to the king's court every day for weeks, but he did not get an opportunity to present himself. Soon, having no source of income or employment, Chiramadeva's money began to run out and he was reduced to eating just one meal a day.

One day, Chiramadeva heard that the raja was going hunting, so he joined the entourage that was accompanying him, hoping to approach him during the hunt. It so happened that in the deepest part of the forest, Raja Gunadhipa became separated from his retainers. When he realized this and looked over his shoulder to see where they were, he saw only one man behind him and he did not even recognize him. Halting his horse, he turned around and asked, 'Who are you? And where is the rest of my retinue?'

'My name is Chiramadeva, Maharaj, and I'm a Rajput. I'm not employed by you, but I'm a part of your hunting party. I was following right behind you; that's why I'm here, while the others are far behind.'

'We'll soon find the others,' Gunadhipa said. 'But tell me, my good man, why do you look so emaciated?'

'To live in a land where the king cares for hundreds and thousands, but somehow overlooks you, is not the king's fault; rather it's the fault of your own stars. The sun shines on everyone and gives light for all to see; if the owl is blind in the day, it's not the sun's fault. Spring season brings greenery to the whole forest; if some trees remain leafless, it's not the fault of spring. In any case, wealth has its own drawbacks. As long as you have it, people remain your friends; once you lose it, your friends, too, leave you. Men who have too much wealth become arrogant. It's better to drink the poison of halahala than to deal with the arrogance of a wealthy man. Wealth, span of life, time of death, learning, and occupation are all determined in the womb. Or, maybe, it's due to karma that the poor remain poor and never benefit from the wealthy. Whatever the cause of my poverty, Maharaj, I'm hoping that by working for you, I'll be able to overcome it.'

The king did not respond to Chiramadeva's insinuation. Instead, he said, 'O Rajput, I'm very hungry. Can you find me some food?'

Chiramadeva was disappointed at the king's disregard in hiring him as a retainer; nevertheless, he immediately began to think of ways to secure food for him. 'Maharaj,' he said, 'it may be difficult to find something to eat in this forest, but I'll try my best.' Then he began searching for fruit trees. The only edible fruit he could find were the sour-tasting amlaka, and he was loath to offer those to anyone, let alone a king. Giving up on fruits, he began to look for game, and finally spotted a deer, which he shot with one accurate arrow. Dragging it to where the king was waiting, he started a fire to roast it.

After Gunadhipa had had a hearty meal, he said to Chiramadeva, 'While you were gone, I looked around to find a way out of the forest, but it appears that we're lost. Can you take me to the city, O Rajput?'

Luckily, Chiramadeva had noticed specific markers in the forest while following Gunadhipa and, using those, he was able to successfully guide Gunadhipa back to the city gates, and from there, he led him to the palace temple. 'Here you are, Maharaj, safely back in your city,' he said to the king, bowing respectfully.

'I'm pleased with your service, Rajput,' Gunadhipa said to him. 'Therefore, I'm employing you. Come to my court tomorrow.'

The following day, the raja rewarded Chiramadeva with a bag of gold coins, expensive clothes, and valuable jewels. And from that day on, Chiramadeva began to work for Raja Gunadhipa.

Once, travelling on some official business on the coast, Chiramadeva came upon a Devi temple on the ocean's bank and stopped to worship there. As he was stepping over the threshold to exit the temple, he saw a beautiful woman at the gate, who was also leaving. She was so alluring that Chiramadeva forgot his business and began to follow her. Sensing someone behind her, the woman stopped and turned around. 'What are you doing here, O Traveller?' she asked Chiramadeva.

'Following you to wherever you lead me. I'm your slave—consumed by desire for you.'

'If you want to fulfil your desire, then bathe in that pool,' she said, pointing to a water tank in the temple's courtyard.

Chiramadeva immediately stripped and dived into the water, but when he emerged, he found that he was no longer on the ocean's bank but standing in his own house in Mithilavati. Dismayed by this magical deportation, Chiramadeva quickly dressed and went to the palace to share his experience with the king. 'I fell in love with the woman, Maharaj,' he declared. 'But sadly, it seems that she rejected me.'

Chiramadeva's account made Raja Gunadhipa very curious to see the magical pool and the mysterious woman, so he gave orders to his men to prepare for his journey to the coast.

Gunadhipa and Chiramadeva then travelled to the coast and Chiramadeva took the king to the Devi temple on the ocean's bank. After offering worship, as they stepped over the threshold into the courtyard outside, they saw a young woman beside them also leaving the temple. Recognizing her, Chiramadeva called out to her. She smiled and came to meet him. When he introduced her to Raja Gunadhipa, she shyly bowed her head and blushed. 'O King,' she said, 'my heart is filled with desire for you. How can I please you? Whatever you say, I'll do.'

'If that is so, then marry Chiramadeva, my Rajput retainer.'

'But I've fallen in love with you, and it's you I desire,' said the woman to Gunadhipa. 'How can I marry someone else?'

'Just now you said that you'd do as I say. Are you now going back on your word?'

The woman shook her head and agreed to marry Chiramadeva. Gunadhipa performed their gandharva nuptials right there and leaving Chiramadeva on the coast with his new bride, returned to Mithilavati.

'O King,' the vetala said to Vikramaditya. 'Tell me, between Raja Gunadhipa and the Rajput Chiramadeva, who is more worthy of praise? Remember, if you know the answer and don't speak it, your head will shatter.'

'Undoubtedly, the Rajput is more praiseworthy,' said Vikramaditya.

'Why do you say that?' asked the vetala. 'Didn't the king generously give up a beautiful woman who loved him and desired him for the sake of his retainer? Then how is it that his retainer is more worthy of praise?'

'What the king did was a gesture worthy of a king. Those whose duty it is to do good to others by virtue of their position cannot be praised for fulfilling their duty. Whereas, the Rajput helped the king when he was not even employed by him. What he did was simply an act of service.'

After hearing these words, the vetala flew back to the shisham tree and the corpse, once again, hung itself from a high branch.

Tale Nine

Who Is More Generous to Madanasena?

'Listen to this strange story, O Raja,' said the vetala to Vikramaditya, as he started back towards the bargad tree with the dead body on his shoulder.

There is a city called Madanapura that was once ruled by Raja Madanavira. In that city lived a very wealthy moneylender called Hiranyagupta, who had a daughter by the name of Madanasena. One day, during the glorious season of Vasant, Madanasena went with her friends to the park to enjoy the pageantry of nature. It so happened that, just then, a young man, Somadatta, who was the businessman Dharmadatta's son, was also in the park with his friends. As he wandered around, he came upon Madanasena in a fragrant grove and fell instantly and madly in love with her. 'Ah! If this woman were to become my wife,' he said to his friends, 'my life's purpose would be fulfilled.'

'A wife fulfils just a single purpose of life,' said one of his friends. 'There are other goals in life as well, my friend.'

'Not for me,' Somadatta said. 'Aside from her, my life has no other goal. In fact, without her my life is of no use.'

In this emotional state, Somadatta approached Madanasena and, taking her hand, passionately declared his love: 'Beautiful maiden, that tikka on your forehead, between your brows, is like the sharp tip of an arrow. Tautening your eyebrows like bowstrings, whom do you plan to strike? If it is I, then you're too late, because I'm already in love with you, and if you don't return my love, I'll give up my life.'

'Please don't do that,' Madanasena cried. 'Your passion and intensity have won me over and I, too, am feeling the sharp arrows of love.'

'Then be my wife,' Somadatta begged.

'I can't. I'm to be wedded to someone else five days from now. He's a businessman's son and his name is Amadatta.'

'That can't be,' Somadatta cried. 'You must refuse. Otherwise, I'll take you by force.'

'Oh no, don't do that. Men who are born in noble families don't force themselves on women, even if their breath is strangled in their throats. They know very well that women are shielded by their modesty and the honour of their family.'

'Fair maiden, an impassioned heart is a hut made of straw that is easily set ablaze. My heart burns for you. In such a situation, who cares what's right and what's wrong? Be mine.'

Madanasena trembled. Caught in the heat of Somadatta's fiery passion, her mind and body became opposing forces. 'Your love is making me forget all propriety and matters of dharma and adharma,' she said. 'But you must allow me some time. I'll come to you myself. After my wedding ceremony, I'll come to you before I go into my husband's embrace. That's my promise to you.'

'Swear that you will?' Somadatta insisted.

'I swear. I'll come to your house on the night of my wedding. Wait for me,' she said.

'I will. My eyes won't blink all night.'

Thus, having made a vow to each other, the two returned to their homes, and five days later, Madanasena was married. Once the nuptial concluded, the groom's sister took Madanasena to her room and adorned her with jewellery, before shepherding her to the flower-fragrant marriage bed and leaving her there to wait for Amadatta. Soon, Amadatta came into the room and, sitting down next to his new bride, reached to embrace her. But Madanasena pushed his hands away.

Amadatta was taken aback. 'Is there a reason for which you are rejecting my embrace?' he asked.

She nodded and told him everything that had transpired between her and Somadatta in the park. 'I made him a promise,' she told her new husband.

'If that is the case, and you want to go to him, then do so,' he said. 'I won't stop you.'

Without a word, Madanasena got up and walked out of the room. By this time, all the wedding guests had left and Amadatta's parents had also gone to sleep; hence, there was no one to question her as she slipped out of the house and into the dark night.

As she was heading to Somadatta's house, a robber saw her. 'What a gift from this dark night,' he said to himself, smiling at the fortuity. 'A lone woman adorned in jewels; what else can a thief ask for?' Slipping out from behind the wall, where he was hiding, he approached Madanasena on quiet feet. 'Beautiful maiden,' he said softly, 'you're walking alone in the night. Where are you going?'

'To my lover,' Madanasena replied, without missing a step.

'Tell me truly,' said the thief. 'Are you not afraid of walking alone in the dark night, dressed as you are? What if you're accosted by thieves and robbers—like me?'

'No, I'm not afraid,' Madanasena replied. 'Kamadeva himself walks beside me, protecting me with his flowered bow and arrows.'

'How so?' the thief asked, and Madanasena told him everything about the promise she had made Somadatta and how her husband had let her go, unimpeded. 'I know you're a thief,' she said. 'But please don't rob me of my jewellery yet. Let me go and meet my beloved, fully adorned. I promise you that on my return, I'll pass this way again. Then I will hand over all my jewels to you myself.'

'Go,' the thief said. 'I wish you a happy union with your lover. But do keep your promise to me.'

Reaching Somadatta's house, Madanasena let herself in quietly and went to his room. He was fast asleep and she had to shake him by the shoulders to awaken him. Suddenly pulled out of sleep, Somadatta woke up confused. He saw a beautiful woman in bridal finery and laden with jewels, standing near his bed, and had no idea who she was. 'Are you a yakshini, or an apsara? Maybe you're a gandharvi or a kinnari; or perhaps, you're a siddha or a vidyadhari. Whoever you are, you're surely a being from either swargaloka or patalaloka. You can't be from this earth.'

'I'm very much of the earth. Don't you know me? I'm Madanasena. Remember, I promised you that I would come to you right after my wedding ceremony, before I accepted my husband's embrace? Now, here I am. Do as you please.'

'Oh!' Somadatta exclaimed, jumping out of bed in surprise. 'You've come.' He had not expected her to keep her promise. 'Does your husband know?'

'Oh yes. I told him everything,'

Somadatta shook his head, perplexed. Women, he thought to himself. Who has ever understood them? They can love you passionately, or they can reject you with a cold heart. They are unpredictable and impetuous, disregarding of propriety, following a path of their own. Intoxicating and even poisonous. They can fill you with joy, or they can destroy you. They can shower love on you, and profess love to another, while they are pining away for someone completely different. What is in their mind is never on their tongue. Capricious, duplicitous, passionate, enticing—women are the downfall of men, no matter who they are. Kings or wise men—all fall prey to this unfathomable creation of the Creator. Thinking these thoughts, Somadatta stepped away from Madanasena. 'You are a married woman now,' he said to her. 'I can't take another man's wife.'

Without a word, Madanasena turned around and left Somadatta's house to return to her husband. She took the same path on her way back and, when she neared the wall, she called out to the thief, 'I'm here. Come and take my jewels, if you wish.'

The thief left the shadows and came to her. 'You're back so early. Did you not see your lover?'

'I did, but he didn't touch me and I'm now returning to my husband. But I've come to keep my promise to you. Should I remove my jewellery?'

The thief shook his head. 'No,' he said. 'I'll not touch your jewels. You are a new bride on her way to meet her husband. But I do commend you for keeping your promise.'

Back in the bridal room with Amadatta, Madanasena related to him everything that had happened. And this is how Amadatta responded: 'A koel's beauty is in her sweet tone, a woman's beauty is in her faithfulness; those who are ugly are made beautiful with learning, and forgiveness is the beauty of an ascetic mind.' Then he took her in his arms and made tender love to her.

'Now answer my question, if you can, King,' the vetala said. 'And, if you've forgotten, let me remind you that if you know the answer and don't give it, your head will be all over this cremation ground in a thousand pieces. The question is this:

who out of the three men in this story is the most generous—the husband, Amadatta; Somadatta, the man Madanasena promised to meet after her wedding; or the thief?

'Clearly, the thief is the most generous,' said Raja Vikramaditya.

'How so?'

'The husband's reason to let her go was that his wife loved another. The lover's reason was that he didn't wish to touch another man's wife, but the robber had no reason at all to let her go. So, out of the three, he is the most selfless and generous.'

With a cackling laugh, the dead body lifted off Raja Vikramaditya's shoulder and flew back to the shisham tree.

Tale Ten

Who Is the Most Delicate Queen?

Vikramaditya returned to the shisham tree and climbed up its crooked trunk to the leafy branch from which the dead body was hanging. Cutting the rope and letting the corpse drop to the ground, he jumped down. Then, lifting it to his shoulder, he began to walk resolutely towards the bargad tree again.

'I applaud you for your persistence, O Raja,' the vetala said. 'You deserve another story. Listen! It's an interesting one.'

In the kingdom of Gaur is the city of Vardhamana. Once upon a time, it was ruled by Raja Gunashekhara, whose minister Abhayachanda was a practising Jain. Often, he would share the philosophies of his faith with Gunashekhara. 'Maharaj,' he would say, 'a person should not do that to others which he himself does not like. Life is impermanent; only death is certain. Man lives and dies repeatedly. That is why a person should do good acts in life and shun greed, anger, lust, and desire. These passions are hard to overcome, but by seeking sanctuary with Jinas, a person can not only overcome them but also gain inner strength and outward grace.'

He would also denigrate Hindu gods and practices: 'Maharaj, the avatars of gods, like Vishnu and Mahadeva, are themselves not passionless,' he would tell the king. 'Therefore, worshipping them or turning to them for guidance leads a person to become even more entangled in the conduct that binds him to samsara. Also know that those who prey upon the poor and get pleasure from watching others in pain are doomed to end up in hell. Those who feed upon the flesh of other creatures to nourish their own flesh are no better than carnivorous beasts; they, too, earn themselves hell. These people are reborn disfigured—maimed, blind, dwarfish. Just as they have eaten the flesh of others, so are their bodies born with missing parts. Eating meat and drinking alcohol are two conducts that endanger a person's well-being in this life and the next.'

In this way, with his persuasive ideology, Abhayachanda indoctrinated the king, who not only became a Jain but also reconstituted the kingdom's laws based on Jain tenets. He sent town-criers into every part of Gaur to forbid people from worshipping Shiva and Vishnu. He also banned gambling and alcohol, and outlawed sacred Hindu dharma rites and rituals, such as Godaan, Bhumidaan, and Pindadaan. People were also prohibited from giving sanctuary to brahmins, yogis, and sanyasis. And if anyone was caught breaking these laws, he was severely punished: his property and wealth were seized by the king, and he was banished from the kingdom.

Then, one day, yielding to the relentless march of Great Time, Gunashekhara passed away, and his son, Dharmadhwaja, succeeded him as king of Gaur. As soon as he came to the throne, Dharmadhwaja threw Abhayachanda out of the kingdom. Amidst jeering crowds and rolling kettledrums, seated backwards on an ass, with his head shaved except for seven tufts that made him look like a fool, the Jain minister was led out of the city.

Henceforth, Raja Dharmadhwaja began to live an indulgent and carefree life with his three wives, Indralekha, Tarawali, and Mrigankavati. One day, in the season of Vasanta, he visited a pleasure garden with his wives. The scenic spring garden was fit for Kamadeva's sport. Its four sides were lined with flower-laden trees. Kooing koels and buzzing bees, speaking the language of love, carried the love-god's messages from flower to flower and tree to tree. In the middle of the garden was a big lake with blooming, colourful lotuses looking like a fragrant rainbow on earth. Dharmadhwaja wandered around with his wives for a while, feeling intoxicated by the sights and sounds of the sensual environment. When they came to the lake's edge, he reached into the water and broke off a pink lotus. Then, turning to his favourite wife Indralekha, he trailed the lotus bloom down her face, from her sea-shell ear to her petal-soft lips. Laughing flirtatiously, Indralekha tried to grab the flower from him, but it slipped from her fingers and landed on her foot. She screamed and fell to the ground, writhing and wailing in pain. Dharmadhwaja shouted for his physicians and they came running. When they examined the queen's foot, they were shocked to discover that it was broken. How could a flower cause a bone to break, they wondered, as they applied cold compresses and put a splint. Then she was put in a palanquin and carried to the palace.

After Indralekha was comfortably settled in her bed, Dharmadhwaja decided to visit his second wife, Tarawali. Her attendant informed him that the queen was resting in the Moon Palace, which was named for its many windows through which the moonlight streamed in. At the bedroom door of this palace, Dharmadhwaja stood watching Tarawali, noticing how enchanting she looked lying on the sandalwood bed. Her body was covered with a fine white silken sheet; her long black tresses, as dark as midnight, were spread in disarray on the pillow; and, in their midst, her face glowed like the moon. Entering the room, Dharmadhwaja sat down beside his queen and lifted her head on his lap to caress her silken tresses. The sheet that was covering her slipped off a little, and a shaft of moonlight struck her bare arm. Tarawali woke up, screaming, 'I'm burning. I'm burning,' and sat up, cradling her arm. When Dharmadhwaja looked down at her arm, he saw a large blister appear on it.

'Beloved, what happened?' Dharmadhwaja asked her.

'The moon's ray burnt me,' she said, sobbing.

Dharmadhwaja immediately called his physicians again. They came quickly and tended to Tarawali's burns with sandalwood paste and other soothing salves, wondering how delicate the queen must be that her skin could not bear even the touch of a moon ray.

Word of the incident spread all over the royal compound, and it also reached the ears of the third queen, Mrigankavati, who was in her room getting dressed. Leaving her toilet midway through, she quickly covered herself with a shawl and went to check on Tarawali. As she stepped out of her palace, she heard the faraway pounding of a pestle. The sound was somewhere in the city and barely perceptible; however, it gave Mrigankavati such a headache that she fainted.

Her attendants brought her back to her room and revived her; then they sent for the king.

'What happened?' Dharmadhwaja asked, rushing in.

'Maharaj, the sound of the pestle has given me a pounding headache,' Mrigankavati replied.

Once again, the king's physicians were summoned, and they came as quickly as they could, equipped with balms and cold compresses to reduce the pain in Mrigankavati's head, feeling amazed at how a faint sound far away could cause such a headache. Surely, the king's wives are the most delicate creatures on earth, they thought to themselves.

'What do you think?' the vetala asked Vikramaditya. 'Out of those three queens, who do you think is the most delicate?'

'The queen who developed a headache and fainted, of course,' said Vikramaditya.

'How so?'

'Because she was the only one who experienced pain without even coming into direct contact with the object that caused her pain.'

Hearing this response, the vetala flew back to the tree, and the dead body, once again, hung itself from a high branch.

Tale Eleven

Why Did the Chief Minister Die at the Celebration of the King's Happiness?

No sooner was Raja Vikram on his way to the bargad tree again than the vetala on his shoulder said to him, 'O Raja, you must be tired from all this toil. Your patience has won me over, and I want to alleviate your tiredness. Let me tell you another story. Listen!'

In Angadesha, there was once a youthful king called Yashaketu, whose beauty rivalled Kamadeva's. He was also a great warrior and his prowess in suppressing enemies was no less than Indra's. This king had a chief minister called Dirghadarshi, who, true to his name, was as farsighted and wise as Brihaspati, the priest of the gods.

One day, Yashaketu said to Dirghadarshi, 'What use are youth and kingdom if they don't facilitate the company of beautiful women. Look at my misfortune; I have beautiful wives, but my kingly duties don't allow me to spend any time with them. Therefore, I've decided to hand over the kingdom to you and devote all my time to my wives.'

Dirghadarshi was aghast. He felt overwhelmed by the responsibility that was suddenly thrust upon him. But he could not refuse the king. Thus, while Yashaketu began to spend his days and nights in the women's palace, immersed in pleasure, his chief minister, Dirghadarshi, began to work from morning till night to manage the affairs of the kingdom. He was efficient and dedicated in his service; however, a king is a king, and a minister is a minister; the latter cannot replace the former. Soon, the people of Angadesha began to notice their raja's continued absence, and rumours spread that Dirghadarshi had somehow persuaded Raja Yashaketu to hand over the kingdom to him so that he could get his hands on the state's wealth. Already under tremendous pressure from the kingdom's work, Dirghadarshi was shattered by this troubling rumour, and his health began to suffer. One day, noticing how haggard he was looking, his wife said to him, 'Why don't you ask the Raja to return to his court?'

'What will I tell him? That I am incapable of taking care of matters? He'll lose all faith in me.'

'I have an idea. Tell him that you want to go on a pilgrimage. He can't refuse you that. Then he'll have to give up his pleasure pursuits and return to his royal duties.'

Taking his wife's advice, Dirghadarshi requested a meeting with the king at the women's palace and said to him, 'Maharaj, lately I've been feeling that I lack dharmic merit, and I fear for my afterlife. Therefore, please give me permission to go on a pilgrimage to gain merit.'

'Won't charity suffice?' Yashaketu asked, loth to give up his life of leisure. 'If you give away wealth to the needy, that, too, earns you merit, does it not?'

'Yes, Maharaj, it does. But going on a pilgrimage at my age is prescribed by the shastras and I want to make this arduous journey before I get too old.'

Yashaketu reluctantly sanctioned the chief minister's request and recommenced the management of the kingdom's affairs. Dirghadarshi happily relinquished his position and set off on his journey. Crossing various rivers and passing through different kingdoms, he visited numerous holy sites and finally arrived in Rameswaram. Here, after bathing and cleansing himself, he first worshipped the Jyotirlinga in the Shiva temple and then sat by the seashore where Shri Rama's armies had created the Rama Setu. As he watched the ocean waves, he witnessed an extraordinary thing: an immense, magical tree suddenly arose from the waters. Its trunk was gold, its leaves were pure emeralds, its flowers were yellow sapphires, and its fruits were red coral. Sitting in the midst of the jewelled branches was the most beautiful woman Dirghadarshi had ever seen. She was playing on the veena and singing in a voice so melodious it could only be described as heavenly. 'Whatever one sows, one reaps,' she sang. 'Once a karma is committed/ it cannot be erased even by the Creator himself.'

When the woman's song came to an end, both she and the tree vanished in the foam. Dirghadarshi sat bemused for some time. Then he quickly gathered his belongings and set off for home.

'I see that you're back,' Yashaketu remarked when he saw Dirghadarshi in the assembly hall on the morning of his return. 'Do tell me about your travels. Where did you go? What all did you see?'

'Maharaj, I visited all the holy sites from here to Rameswaram, where Shri Rama's monkey army created the bridge over the ocean. But, as I was sitting there, thinking about Shri Rama, I saw something that was absolutely incomprehensible and inconceivable. The wise say one should not speak about things that are incomprehensible or inconceivable. But what if one witnesses such a sight?'

'Tell me in detail what you saw,' the king urged.

'Maharaj, I saw a marvellous tree rise from the waters. Its trunk was as wide as a mountainside, and its branches were laden with leaves, flowers, and fruits. But none of these was of the ordinary kind; the trunk was pure gold, the leaves were pure emeralds, the flowers were yellow sapphire gems, and the fruits were red coral. And that's not all. Sitting in the middle of all the gold and gems was a woman more beautiful than any I've seen. She was playing the veena and singing in a heavenly voice. As soon as she stopped singing, she and the tree vanished into the ocean, as though they had never existed.'

Listening to Dirghadarshi, Yashaketu felt a compelling desire to visit Rameswaram and see the magical woman in the jewelled tree. 'I must see this astonishing sight,' he said to Dirghadarshi. 'In fact, I feel that if I don't witness it myself, I'll die of curiosity. Please take care of the kingdom while I'm gone.'

The very next morning, Yashaketu left for Rameswaram, and, once again, Dirghadarshi found himself shouldering the weight of the kingdom, wondering how long he would have to bear the burden this time.

Yashaketu was in a hurry to see the woman in the tree. Like his chief minister, he, too, crossed many rivers and passed through several kingdoms, but unlike Dirghadarshi, he did not stop at any of the sacred pilgrimage sights; his goal was only the seashore at Rameswaram. Once there, he worshipped at the Shiva temple, and then sat down on the ocean's bank, impatiently awaiting the golden, jewelled tree with the beautiful, singing maiden. Before long, the tree appeared and it was exactly as his minister had described—made of gold, laden with emerald leaves, sapphire flowers, and red coral fruits, and sitting on it was an apsara-like woman, playing the veena and singing in a divine voice. Even though Yashaketu had been expecting this vision, the miracle of it still stunned him. Then the woman stopped singing, and both she and the tree disappeared in the waves. Without a second thought, Yashaketu dived into the ocean and began looking for the tree all around, but there was no sign of it. He went deeper and deeper, till his breathing became laboured, and his limbs began to get heavy. When he was on the verge of giving up, a strong force suddenly pulled him from below, and he lost consciousness. When he opened his eyes again, he found himself inside a city of unimaginable opulence. Its walls were made of gold and its pillars were studded with gems. The houses, too, had golden walls, and windows with curtains made of strung pearls. All around were gardens full of lush, bejewelled, wish-fulfilling trees, and gem-lined ponds filled with lotuses of all hues. However, there was an unnatural silence everywhere; not a soul was in sight. Even the houses were all unpeopled. Yashaketu walked down several streets, looking for someone to talk to. At the end of one of the streets, he came to a palace that was shimmering with thousands of gems studded in its walls. Climbing the stairs, he entered the great hall, but here, too, not a single being was in sight. At the end of the assembly hall was a line of doors, which he began to open one by one, only to discover that each one led to a room as empty as the city. Then he opened the last door, and his heart jumped with joy, for in that room was a bed in which the woman from the tree was lying. As soon as Yashaketu entered the room, she opened her eyes and sat up. 'Who are you,' she asked in a melodious voice, 'and how did you get to this underwater city where no man has ever come before?'

'O beautiful lady, I'm the king of Angadesha, and my love for you has brought me to your underwater city. Please, tell me, who are you?'

'All I can tell you right now is that my name is Mrigankavati. The rest I'll reveal in good time,' she replied.

'Marry me,' the king said. 'I've fallen in love with you and can't live without you.'

'If that is what you want, then, yes, I'll marry you, but you'll have to a make me a promise that you'll never approach me on the fourteenth day of the dark half of the month.'

'You have my promise,' Yashaketu replied.

Then the two of them tied the nuptial knot in a gandharva marriage and began to live happily in Mrigankavati's underwater palace. They spent all night wrapped in each other's arms and, during the day, they wandered, hand-in-hand, in the empty streets and lush gardens. They bathed in the lotus lake whenever they wished and they used the wish-granting kalpavrikshas to fulfil their needs. Then the fourteenth night of the dark half of the month arrived and the woman said to Yashaketu, 'Today, you will not approach me. You must go.'

Yashaketu was loth to leave her, but he nodded and got up to exit the room. But, when he reached the door, he opened it and shut it without stepping out. Then, tiptoeing to a dark corner, he hid there, very curious to see why his wife wanted to be alone on this night.

At midnight, Yashaketu heard a loud rumble, as though the walls of the palace were cracking, and then he saw a huge, ugly rakshasa with bloodshot eyes, wild hair, and big, yellow teeth enter the room. Lumbering towards Mrigankavati's bed, he grabbed her and thrust her into his mouth and swallowed her whole in one gulp.

Yashaketu pulled out his sword in rage and rushed toward the rakshasa. Leaping up, he swiped the blade clean through his neck. The rakshasa's head fell to the floor with a thud, followed by his body, which crashed with such force that the whole palace shook. Yashaketu then carefully cut the rakshasa's belly and helped his beloved climb out.

'O brave one, you have done me a great favour today,' Mrigankavati cried, falling into Yashaketu's arms. 'It is true when they say that every forest doesn't have sandalwood, every tusker's head is not crested with a pearl, every mountain doesn't have emeralds, and every city doesn't have brave men. You, my dear one, are the bravest of the brave.'

'Who was this rakshasa and why did he eat you?' Yashaketu asked. 'And why did you forbid me from approaching you on this fourteenth day of the dark half of the month?'

'Brave one, today I'll tell you my story. Listen! My father is the king of vidyadharas. His name is Mrigankasena. That's why my name is Mrigankavati. My father loved me very much; he wouldn't even eat the evening meal unless I was sitting beside him. Once, on the fourteenth day of the dark fortnight, I was engaged in some long rituals of worship, and I lost track of time. The hour of the evening meal arrived and passed, and my father kept waiting for me. He didn't eat that day; the only thing that fed his belly was anger. When I returned home, he was so angry that he cursed me: "For the rest of your immortal life, on every fourteenth night of the dark half of the month, you'll be swallowed by the rakshasa Kritantasantrasa. You'll always manage to tear your way out of his belly, but it'll repair right after, and he'll become whole again and swallow you again on the same day of the next month." So, you see, ever since I was cursed, this night has been repeating every month. This underwater palace is also a part of the curse. I was to live here by myself, away from my vidyadhara community, forever; however, once my father's anger dissipated, he reduced the severity of the curse. "If a brave man kills the rakshasa, you'll be freed," he said to me. And I've been seeking such a man for years. Many men have seen me at the seashore, but none has dared to jump into the ocean to find me, and certainly no one has attempted to kill Kritantasantrasa. But now you have done so and I'm free. I'm very grateful to you. Now, I must return to my father and his land, where I belong. You can stay here as long as you wish. I gift this palace to you as a reward for your bravery.'

Yashaketu was heartbroken at the thought of losing his Mrigankavati. 'Before you leave for your father's land, can I request you to fulfil my desire?' he asked.

'Yes,' she nodded.

'I want you to come and visit my kingdom of Angadesha before you go to your land. I want you to see it just once. Come and stay there with me for seven days.'

'Alright,' Mrigankavati said and, taking Yashaketu by the hand, led him to a spot behind the palace that was overgrown and unkempt. In the midst of it was a pond that was hardly visible. 'By taking a dip in this pond, we'll be able to get to the human world,' she said.

'But it looks abandoned,' Yashaketu said.

'That's because it has never been used, but trust me, it works,' Mrigankavati replied, and, clasping his hand, jumped into the water. In his next breath, Yashaketu was in Angadesha, standing in his room in the royal palace and beside him was his beloved Mrigankavati.

The minister, Dirghadarshi, was so happy to hear that the king had returned that he arranged for festivities throughout the kingdom. Streets were decorated with colourful flags and strings of scented flowers. Five kinds of drums played in the streets, calling the citizens to come out of their homes and dance and sing to welcome their raja. Bards and minstrels sang Yashaketu's praises, and Vedic brahmins performed yajnas, chanting mantras of purification and felicitation.

Mrigankavati stayed with Yashaketu for seven days. On

the eighth morning, she said to him, 'I must go to my father now. Please understand. Vidyadhara law forbids me to stay with a mortal.'

Yashaketu nodded and held her in one last embrace. Mrigankavati, too, was sad. With tears flowing down her cheeks, she placed her head on his heart and bade him farewell. Then, disengaging herself from his arms, she sat down to say the mantra that would transport her to her father's land. However, nothing happened. Mrigankavati repeated the mantra several times, but her body didn't budge.

'What has happened?' Yashaketu asked, hardly able to contain his excitement. 'Are your mantras not able to take you back?'

'It seems that I've become human,' she said, puzzled. 'I think, staying with you, living like a human, and thinking and feeling like a human have superseded my magical vidyadhara powers. Now, I can't go back. I must stay on this earth like an ordinary human.'

Yashaketu scooped Mrigankavati into his arms. 'O my beloved, I'm so happy,' he cried. Then he called Dirghadarshi to order a second celebration in the kingdom. Following his orders, Dirghadarshi made the necessary arrangements. When the citizens of Angadesha began to celebrate again, Dirghadarshi's heart burst in his chest, and he died.

'Tell me, O King,' said the vetala to Raja Vikramaditya, 'why did the chief minister die as soon as the second celebration started? Was it because he was jealous that the king had acquired the woman of heavenly beauty? Tell me the answer, and if you don't, your head will become a thousand pieces.'

'I know the answer,' Vikramaditya said. 'The chief minister died because he was true at heart. He had already witnessed once how the king abandoned the kingdom and its welfare when he was immersed in pleasures with his wives. Therefore, the second celebration indicated that he was going down the same path again, and this time, it was going to be worse, because the new wife was a woman of heavenly beauty.'

As soon as the vetala heard this answer, the dead body on Raja Vikramaditya's shoulder flew to the shisham tree.

Tale Twelve

Who Is Responsible for Hariswami's Death?

Taking the corpse down from the shisham tree, Vikramaditya settled it on his shoulder again. When he started walking toward the bargad tree, the vetala said: 'O Raja, here is a short tale for your entertainment.'

There is a city called Chudapura that was named after its king, Chudamana. The king's guru was a brahmin called Devaswami, and he had a son whose name was Hariswami. This young man had the looks of Kamadeva, the brains of Brihaspati, and the wealth of Kubera, and he was married to Lavanyavati—a woman whose beauty paralleled that of the apsara Tilottama. Their marriage was very successful, because not only were they well matched, but they were also deeply in love.

One summer night, lying on the roof, Lavanyavati and Hariswami made love and then fell asleep, still unclothed. A vidyadhara, who was flying across the night sky, saw the naked beauty of Lavanyavati and was captivated. Swooping down, he grabbed her, put her in his flying chariot, and took off for his celestial palace. When Hariswami woke up in the middle of the night, he found that his wife was not by his side. Getting up, he began looking for her. First, he checked all around the roof and then went downstairs and searched in every single room of the house. Not finding her anywhere, he went to search in the garden. 'Where could she have gone?' he kept asking himself, hurrying along the garden paths, peering into every shadow. 'Is she angry with me? Maybe she's gone to a friend's house? But why would she do that in the middle of the night?' Unable to find her, he finally sat down, right there in the garden, and spent the remainder of the night worrying himself sick and praying to the gods for her well-being. The elements of the night became his love's messengers. When a gentle breeze fanned him like a caress, he said to it, 'O gentle breeze, go and caress her first. Then come back to me with the same caress. I may die in this separation.' And when a night bird chirped to express its love for the moon, his eyes became moist. 'O bird,' he said to it, 'go and profess my love to my beloved before you sing love songs to the moon.'

As the night's darkness began to dispel with still no sign of Lavanyavati, Hariswami began to despair: 'Oh my beloved,' he wailed, 'my wife with a face as attractive as the moon, with a body as fair-complexioned as the moon, where are you? Did the night steal you in envy of your beauty? This moon that used to shed its coolness on me when I was in your company, now burns me in your absence; every drop of moonlight falls on me like a live ember. I can't bear the pain.'

Then the sun dawned, and the world brightened into day, but Hariswami's heart was steeped in darkness. All that day and the next, he searched for her in every corner of the city, only to return home dejected. After that, for days, he sat in the house, weeping in sorrow. His friends and relatives tried to console him: 'Why are you lamenting her as though she's dead?' they said. 'She's not dead. She'll surely return to you. Don't lose hope. Be patient.'

Days passed, and finally Hariswami gained some fortitude, but it left him feeling disenchanted with his world. 'What's the use of this life?' he asked himself. 'Why do I need all this wealth and creature comforts?' Hence, he decided to give it all up and go on a pilgrimage to spend time with holy men, sadhus, and brahmins. 'That'll help me cleanse some sins,' he rationalized. 'Perhaps, it'll also make me more deserving of my beloved and she'll return to me.'

Giving away all his wealth in charity, he donned the garb of a renunciant, and wearing just a loincloth and bead necklaces, set off on the journey to sacred sites. Even when the season changed, and the sun, like a roaring lion with a ruddy mane, began to bear down on the world, Hariswami continued to travel from city to town to village. One afternoon, suffering the ravages of the weather, he arrived in a town with his throat parched, his body scorched, and his stomach caving inwards with hunger. 'I must get some food and shelter before I die,' he said to himself, and, tamping down on the shame he felt at having to beg, quickly made a bowl from palash leaves and knocked at the first door he came to. When a man is wracked with creature needs of the body, he doesn't think of his status, honour, or even caste. The only thing that matters at that time is survival. Fortunately for him, the house he was at belonged to a brahmin. As soon as the man answered the door, Hariswami requested him to give him some food, and the brahmin summoned his wife. She came with a jug of kheer and poured some of it into his bowl of leaves.

Thanking her, Hariswami hurried to a river to cleanse himself before eating and, seeing a bargad tree on the bank, set the bowl in its roots. As he was washing, a hawk, carrying a freshly killed snake in its beak, landed on a branch of the bargad tree, just above the bowl. The snake hung limply from the bird's beak, and the poison from its fangs dripped into the bowl of kheer.

After completing his ablutions, Hariswami came to the

bargad tree, picked up the bowl, and sat down in its shade to eat the kheer. Just as he was finishing it, his insides began to burn. Oh, when Great Time itself is unfavourable, even the sweetness of kheer can turn poisonous, he thought and, staggering to his feet, managed to walk to the brahmin's house. This time, when he knocked, the brahmin's wife opened the door. 'O brahmini,' he said to her, 'your kheer has turned to poison in my body. Quickly arrange for some anti-venom herbs to save me, or you'll be charged with the sin of killing a brahmin.'

The woman called a servant, but before the man could arrive, Hariswami passed away. By this time, the brahmin had also come to the scene. Seeing the dead brahmin at his doorstep, he was horrified. Turning on his wife in anger, he shouted, 'You killed him. It was the food from your hand that did it. You've brought the sin of brahmanicide upon us. Leave my house this instant. I'll have nothing to do with you.' Then he pushed her out of the house and shut the door.

'So, King,' the vetala said to Vikramaditya, 'the brahmin's wife was punished for this sin, but who do you think is really at fault? Who should be held responsible for Hariswami's death? The snake, the hawk, the brahmin's wife, or the brahmin? Who incurred the sin of brahmanicide?'

'It isn't the snake,' Vikramaditya replied. 'It's the nature of snakes to release poison, so how can he be blamed; besides, he was helpless himself, at the mercy of the hawk. But it isn't the hawk, either; he was just satisfying his hunger. Even the brahmin's wife is not responsible because she was simply following her husband's order; she gave the man kheer without any ill intentions. And it is also not the brahmin's fault, even though his wife gave Hariswami the kheer on his behest. He was fulfilling his duty of honouring a guest by giving him food.

So, who incurred the sin of brahmanicide? My answer is—none of them. In fact, the one who puts the blame on another is the one who incurs the sin.'

A cackling laugh shook the body on Vikramaditya's shoulder. Then, it stiffened and, like an arrow, shot through the air and hung itself from the shisham tree. Undeterred, Raja Vikramaditya began walking in that direction again.

Tale Thirteen

Why Did the Robber Cry and Laugh Before His Execution?

'O Raja, you must be exhausted. I'll tell you another strange tale to distract you from your toil,' the vetala said once Vikramaditya had the corpse back on his shoulder.

There is a city called Chandrudaya, where a king called Randhir used to rule. He cared deeply for his subjects, and he did everything in his power to protect them and keep them happy. In that city also lived a very rich merchant called Dharmadhwaja, and he had a daughter called Kshobhini. The girl was so beautiful that the sun envied her glow and the moon envied her grace. As she grew older, her beauty also grew, and her acclamation brought a number of suitors, including princes and kings. However, Kshobhini refused to marry. Dharmadhwaja was greatly distressed at his daughter's decision, but there was nothing he could do to deter her; all he could do was hope that, one day, she would change her mind.

Once, it so happened that the city of Chandrudaya became a nexus for robbers. Every night, homes were robbed and businesses were looted. Fed up with this sudden escalation in crime, the citizens of Chandrudaya petitioned the king. 'Maharaj,' they complained, 'every night there are several robberies in the city, yet no one has ever seen the robbers. And not one of them has been apprehended. We are requesting you to please do something about this.'

The king was deeply concerned to hear about the situation and took immediate action. He installed a secret night watch throughout the city, with guardsmen disguised as ordinary citizens patrolling the streets from sunset to sunrise. However, contrary to the king's expectation, this measure hardly served as a deterrent; the robbers still remained at large and the robberies continued unabated. Finally, the king decided to get personally involved. Dismissing the patrolmen, he took up the night watch himself and, armed with his sword and shield, began to patrol the streets of the city. One night, he saw a man walking stealthily, keeping to the shadows, and constantly looking over his shoulder. Seeing his suspicious behaviour, Raja Randhir deliberately walked towards him and called out, 'Who are you?'

'I'm a thief,' replied the man. 'Who are you?'

'I, too, am a thief,' said the king.

The thief laughed merrily. 'Well met, friend,' he said. 'Fate has brought us together. Come, let's join forces.'

'All right,' said the king and, for the rest of the night, he worked as the thief's accomplice as he went from house to house, stealing whatever he could. At daybreak, the thief took Raja Randhir to the outskirts of the city, where there was a large well, and, gesturing to him to follow him, began to descend into the well. Curious to see where the thief would lead him, Raja Randhir followed him down the steps that were notched into the side of the well. When Randhir reached the bottom of the well, he found himself standing beside the thief, outside the gates of an underground mansion. 'Wait here, I'll be right back,' the thief said to him and slipped in through the gates.

As Raja Randhir waited, the gate opened, and a maid came out. Seeing the king standing there, she stopped in her tracks. Then, drawing closer to him, she asked in a whisper, 'What are you doing here, Maharaj? Don't you know who lives here?'

'I know,' the king replied. 'That's why I'm here. But he doesn't know who I am. When he comes out, I'll catch him.'

'When he comes out, he'll kill you. That's his intention. Please leave as quickly as you can. Think of your people. Who will help them if you are dead? You can't catch him all by yourself,' the maid advised.

The king saw the wisdom of her words and decided that it was best to leave. Climbing out of the well, he returned to his palace. The following night, taking a strong force of soldiers with him, he went to the thief's mansion through the well and surrounded it. When the robber realized that he was trapped, he came out, brandishing a sword. He battled all the king's soldiers and, single-handedly, destroyed much of the force. Then he began to duel with Raja Randhir. They started with swords, and when they lost those in the fight, they fell upon each other, wrestling. It was a tough combat but, finally, Raja Randhir was able to overpower the robber.

Binding him with strong ropes, the raja's remaining men dragged the robber out of the well and into the palace's dungeon. He was kept there for a few days, while arrangements were made for his crucifixion. On the day of his execution, the robber was led through the city with town-criers and kettledrums announcing his capture and execution. Hearing those sounds, Kshobhini, the businessman's daughter, came to her window to see what was going on. When she saw the thief in ropes, his muscular body covered in blood and dust, something happened to her. Her legs started shaking, her body flushed, and her heartbeat increased. 'Who is that man?' she asked her maid in a trembling voice.

'That's the robber who was plaguing this city,' the maid replied. 'The king's soldiers are taking him to be executed.'

With a sob, Kshobhini ran to her father. 'Save him,' she begged. 'That's the man I want to marry.'

'Which man, Daughter?'

'That robber who is to be executed—I love him. He's the man I'll marry. Please save him, Father.'

'What are you saying, Daughter?' Dharmadhwaja was flabbergasted. 'That man has been robbing the citizens of Chandrudaya. How can you be in love with a man like that? Besides, the king has already pronounced his punishment. How can I save him?'

'Please, Father,' the girl fell down, sobbing. 'You must. I swear I'll not marry any other man. I love him so much that if he's crucified, I'll burn myself on his pyre.'

Dharmadhwaja loved his daughter very much and her happiness meant everything to him; hence, he had no choice but to give in to her wish. Going to the king, he said, 'Maharaj, I'll give you five lakh gold coins in exchange for the robber's life.' He was, in fact, willing to sacrifice all his wealth if that was what the king demanded to stop the man's execution.

'That man has been plundering my capital,' the king replied. 'He has been looting my people for weeks. To catch him, I had to put my own life in danger. And now you're telling me to just let him go? No, I will not. Not even for all the wealth in the world.'

When Dharmadhwaja returned home and told Kshobhini that he had failed to get the man released, she ran to her room and threw herself down on her bed, sobbing and wailing. After some time, she got up, took a cleansing bath, and, leaving the house, began to walk in the direction of the maidan where the crucifix was being erected. Some of her attendants tried to stop her, while others ran to her parents to inform them. Dharmadhwaja and his wife rushed out of the house, calling after her, begging her to return home, but she was resolute.

When Kshobhini, and her parents and attendants arrived at the execution site, the robber was already raised on the crucifix. Even though his mind was clouded with pain, he saw Kshobini and was taken by her. 'Oh, what a beautiful woman that is,' he said to himself. 'But why is she here and why are her old parents and attendants crying?' Calling out to one of the soldiers in charge of his crucifixion, he asked him who they were.

'That beautiful maiden is Kshobhini, and that old man is her father, Seth Dharmadhwaja. When you were being paraded through the city with the kettledrum, she saw you from a window of her mansion, fell madly in love with you, and swore that she would only marry you and no one else. Her father tried to stop your execution by promising the raja a large sum in exchange for your life, but he refused.'

Hearing this, the robber's eyes filled with tears, and he wept. Then, suddenly, he burst out laughing. And soon after, he died.

Kshobhini had a pyre built for the robber. When he was laid on it, she climbed up and sat down next to his body, taking his head on her lap. When the pyre was lit, her parents and attendants wailed, begging her to give up her quest. But she remained seated, undeterred. Suddenly, to everyone's amazement, the Devi from the nearby temple became manifest. 'Dear child,' she said to Kshobhini, 'I am pleased with your determination and resolve. Ask me for a boon.'

'Devi, if you are pleased with me, then restore this man's life, because I love him.'

'Granted!' said the Devi and summoned a cup of elixir from the bottom of the ocean. As soon as it appeared in her hand, she gave it to Kshobhini and disappeared. Kshobhini poured a few drops of the elixir into the dead robber's mouth. He instantly opened his eyes and stood up, whole and unhurt. Then, taking Kshobhini by the hand, he stepped off the pyre.

Dharmadhwaja was ecstatic to see this miracle, and he profusely thanked the Devi, promising to build a temple for her in that maidan. Kshobhini and the robber were soon married, and the robber swore that he would never rob again. Accepting his word, the king employed him in his service.

'And this is how Kshobhini and the thief started a happy married life,' the vetala said to Vikramaditya. 'Now, let me ask you a question, but first let me remind you that if you don't give me an answer, your head will split into a thousand pieces.'

'What's the question?'

'Why did the robber cry when he heard about the young woman who was willing to die with him? And then, why did he laugh?'

'He cried because he thought how ironic it was that this beautiful woman should fall in love with him at the moment of his death. And he laughed at the irony of the divine plan: the goddess Lakshmi bestows wealth to one who has no talents; Saraswati, goddess of art and music, becomes benevolent to one who is uncouth and crass. Indra, the god of rain, sends down torrents on mountains, and fools, somehow, manage to marry the most beautiful women.'

Hearing Vikramaditya's answer, the vetala flew off his shoulder, and the corpse went and reattached itself to the branch of the shisham tree.

Tale Fourteen

Whose Wife Is She?
A Tale of Switched Genders

Raja Vikramaditya made his way back to the shisham tree. Then, with practised efficiency, he climbed it, cut the corpse loose, jumped to the ground, and hefted the dead body on his shoulder.

'You truly are a determined man,' the vetala said. 'I'm going to tell you a very strange tale. Listen!'

There is a city, Kusumavati. A king named Munivichara once ruled from there. He had a daughter whose name was Chandraprabha, and she was beautiful and radiant like her name.

One spring day, when buds had just begun to flower and soft breezes were just beginning to turn fragrant, Chandraprabha went to the park with her friends. By coincidence, at that time, a brahmin businessman's son, Manasvi, who was as handsome as Kamadeva, was also there, sleeping in the shade of a tree. Skipping around and enjoying the park and each other's company, the young women did not notice the sleeping man. But the sound of their laughter awakened him. He jumped to his feet and suddenly came face to face with the princess. She was just as surprised to see him as he was to see her. When their eyes met, Kamadeva released his arrows and struck them both with such force that Manasvi was knocked unconscious and Chandraprabha's legs gave way under her. She would have fallen if her friends had not caught her.

The princess and her attendants quickly left in their palanquins, but Manasvi lay senseless on the ground. Some time later, two brahmins, Mooladeva and Shashi, happened to come that way. Seeing Manasvi's prone figure, Mooladeva said to his friend, 'Why do you think this handsome youth is lying senseless on the ground?'

'More than likely, it's a woman's doing. She used the bow of her brows to paralyse him with the sharp arrows of her gaze. It's strange how an intelligent man prides himself on his intelligence till the arrows of blue-lotus eyes from under bow-like brows shoot him down.'

'Should we revive him?' Mooladeva asked.

'What's the use?' said his friend, Shashi.

Shaking his head at his friend's lack of concern, Mooladeva took some water in the cup of his hand and sprinkled it on Manasvi's face. Jolted into consciousness, he quickly sat up. But when he saw two men standing before him instead of the woman he wanted to see, he began to wail.

'Why are you crying?' Mooladeva asked him. 'And why were you lying unconscious? What happened to you?'

'Sorrows should only be shared with those who can alleviate them,' he replied.

'Can we be of any help?' Mooladeva asked.

'Sure. Bring me wood for a pyre.'

'Don't talk like that,' Mooladeva chided. 'Tell us the reason for your sorrow. Maybe we can help you.'

'The princess was here in this park with her friends, and when I saw her, I was so overwhelmed with love for her that I lost my senses. I can't live without her. If I don't get her, I'll kill myself. I must make her mine.'

'That may be difficult, but I think we can help you. Come with us to our house. We'll think of a way to take you to the princess. And if we can't, we'll give you a lot of money to help you get over her and find happiness with someone else.'

'I don't want to get over her, and I don't want your money. God has created many kinds of gems, but the best gem is woman. Men desire money only to make a woman happy. If the woman is gone, what use is the money? Even animals are better off than a man without a woman. Dharma begets money, money begets woman, and woman begets happiness; without a woman, there is no happiness in a man's life. And my happiness is only the princess. I must acquire her, or I'll surely die.'

'In that case, I'll get you inside the princess' room,' Mooladeva said. 'The rest is up to you.'

'I'll do anything,' Manasvi said.

Bringing him to his house, Mooladeva fed him and then began to prepare two tiny mantra balls. Once they were ready, he sat down facing Manasvi and explained to him: 'One of these balls is for you, and the other is for me. When you put your ball in your mouth, you'll become a young maiden, and when you take it out, you'll be yourself again.'

'And the other?' Manasvi asked.

'Watch,' Mooladeva said and placed a ball in his own mouth. Instantly, he became a white-haired, wrinkled, octogenarian brahmin. Then he took the other ball and placed it in Manasvi's mouth. Instantly, the handsome brahmin was transformed into a beautiful pubescent maiden. 'Come. Let's go meet the princess,' Mooladeva said, and the two of them went to the palace, where Mooladeva requested a meeting with the king.

Raja Munivichara welcomed the old brahmin with due respect and offered him and the young maiden accompanying him comfortable seats. 'Please tell me, what is your concern?' he asked.

Thanking the king, Mooladeva began to shower benedictions on him: 'He who is glorious in all three worlds, he who took the form of a dwarf to defeat the powerful Bali, he who bridged the great ocean with the help of a monkey army, he who held a mountain aloft on his little finger and saved the cowherds from Indra's fury, may he always protect you!'

The king bowed and then asked the brahmin again, 'O holy man, please tell me where you are from and how can I be of assistance?'

'My home is on the other side of Ganga River,' Mooladeva began. 'I have a son who is twenty years old; this young maiden with me is my son's new bride. She was visiting her parents after the nuptials, and I went to fetch her. But when I returned to my home, I discovered that in my absence, some robbers had raided the whole village and everyone had fled, including my wife and son. I have to go and search for them, but I need to first make sure that my daughter-in-law is safe. That's why I've brought her here, Maharaj. Please keep my son's bride safe in the palace while I look for my wife and son.'

Munivichara looked at the exceptionally beautiful maiden and was reluctant to take her responsibility, worried that if anything happened to her, he would have to face the ire of the brahmin. But then he thought that if he refused the brahmin, the old man may take it as an insult and curse him. Therefore, he agreed. 'I'll keep your daughter-in-law safe till your return,' he promised the old brahmin and summoned his daughter.

When the princess arrived, the king introduced the young maiden to her and instructed her, 'From today, this brahmin's daughter-in-law is your responsibility. Keep her with you every moment of the day. Eating, sleeping, walking, sporting—no matter what you do, be with her at all times. Never be separate from her.'

The princess brought the young maiden to her rooms and did as her father had asked. She never let her out of her sight, so much so that she even shared her bed with her. Before long, the princess and the maiden became fast friends. One day, lying in bed, the brahmin's daughter-in-law asked the princess, 'Why are you always so sad and dejected? It's like you don't enjoy anything in life.'

'One obtains a beloved after much difficulty. Once obtained, love and happiness fill one's life. But what if one's love is lost?' the princess said with a deep sigh. 'O Shiva,' she continued, 'don't create the world, and if you must, then don't create human lives, and if you must, then don't create the experience of love, and if you must, then don't create separation.'

'Tell me what has happened to you,' the daughter-in-law said. 'It's true that no one can grieve for another, but I hear that by sharing grief, you can lessen it.'

'One spring day, I lost all enjoyment of life. I saw a man in the park who was like an incarnation of Kamadeva, and I was struck with such force that it stunned me. I would have fallen to the ground, if my attendants hadn't caught me. Ever since then, I can't eat, I can't sleep. I can only pine for him—day and night. But I don't even know his name or where he lives.'

'What if I help you meet him again? What will you give me in return?' the brahmin's daughter-in-law asked.

'I'll be your slave for the rest of my life.'

The brahmin's daughter-in-law sat up and took out the mantra ball from her mouth. Instantly, she became the young brahmin that the princess had seen in the park.

The princess was dumbstruck to see the woman with whom she had been sharing her private room, bed, and most intimate secrets turn into a male. But she was so ecstatic at the sight of the man she loved that all other thoughts fled her mind. 'How...what....' she began to say. And then finally asked, 'Why?'

'I had to find a way to see you again,' the brahmin replied. 'Or I would have died.'

They fell into each other's arms and cried with joy. Then, performing a gandharva marriage, they swore to never be parted and spent the night in heated, blissful embraces. The next morning, the brahmin woke up before any of the princess' attendants and quickly slipped the ball into his mouth to become a woman again. Henceforth, this became the pattern of life for the princess and the brahmin: lovers during the night and girlfriends during the day. In this way, six months passed. Then the princess became pregnant.

One day, the king was invited to a feast at his chief minister's house, and he took his daughter and the brahmin's daughter-in-law with him. The minister had a son, who was married but did not desire his wife. As soon as he saw the beautiful young woman who had come with the princess, he was struck so gravely with arrows of desire that he lost all colour and his body began to shake. Reeling and staggering, he somehow made it to his room and lay down, sending word to his father that he was unwell and would not be able to join the feast.

Once the feast was over, the minister went to check on his son. Seeing him lying in bed, trembling and moaning, he became worried. 'What has happened to you, Son?' he asked.

'I'm on the verge of death,' the minister's son replied. 'When I saw that woman, who came with the princess, Kamadeva emptied his whole quiver of arrows into my heart. I could hardly bear it. I must acquire that maiden, Father. If I don't, I'll die. Please go to the raja tomorrow and ask for that woman. And if you return with a refusal, be prepared to lay me on a pyre.'

The chief minister went to the king the very next morning and asked him for the woman's hand in marriage for his son.

'It can't be,' said the king, vehemently shaking his head. 'It's against dharma. Not only is she entrusted to me but also she's a married woman.'

'Maharaj, my son will die if he can't have that woman. And if he dies, I, too, will give up my life. I can't live without my son.'

When Raja Munivichara's council heard this exchange, they advised the king: 'If the boy dies, your chief minister will pass away from grief. In that case, who'll manage the administration? Without proper administration, the kingdom will become unstable and your people will suffer. Therefore, Maharaj, you must ensure that the chief minister remains hale and hearty. As for the brahmin and his daughter-in law, it has been six months since that old brahmin left the maiden with you; there has been no communication from the man. Who knows if he's even alive? Therefore, the young maiden he placed in your care is now yours to give away, if you so please. You should marry her to the minister's son to save the kingdom.'

The king was persuaded, and summoning the brahmin's daughter-in-law, he informed her that she would soon be married to the chief minister's son.

'What are you saying, Maharaj?' the maiden cried in panic. 'I'm married. How can I marry another? This is against dharma.'

'Nothing is more important than the dharma of serving the kingdom. Your marriage to my minister's son is imperative for the welfare of this kingdom.'

'If this is the case, then I have no choice, but I do have a condition. I'm a brahmin's daughter; the chief minister's son is a kshatriya. If he wants to marry me, he needs to purify himself by completing a pilgrimage of all the holy sites. Only then will I marry him.'

When the chief minister's son was informed about this condition, he agreed to it, but only if the woman married him before he left.

Manasvi, the brahmin, could not object to that without angering the king, so he agreed. Gathering his womanly belongings and bidding a tearful goodbye to the princess, he went to the chief minister's house as his son's second wife. There, he met the first wife, whose name was Saubhagyasundari.

With the chief minister's son away on pilgrimage, Manasvi, the pretend-wife, and Saubhagyasundari, the real wife, were often in each other's company and they became very good friends. Soon, they were spending all day together and before long, they began to sleep in the same bed, talking till the wee hours of the morning. One day, Saubhagyasundari said to Manasvi, 'With one's husband out of town, what does one do about the fire of desire? Every day I burn. Oh, what agony is this? What sins have I committed to have to bear this?'

'What if I can alleviate your suffering?' Manasvi said. 'What will you give me in exchange?'

'I'll be your slave for the rest of my life.'

Manasvi, the woman, then reached into her mouth and removed the mantra ball. Instantly, she became a handsome young man. From that night on, the first wife, Saubhagyasundari, and Manasvi, the brahmin, began to live as lovers at night and co-wives during the day.

In this way, another six months passed. Then the minister's household received news that the son was returning home from the pilgrimage, and the family began to prepare for a festive celebration to welcome him. Everyone was excited about his arrival, except Manasvi, who wondered what he would do when the husband came to his bed. Then an idea came to him. Removing the ball from his mouth, he quietly left the house, without anyone noticing, and went to see Mooladeva.

'I don't know what to do,' he said to Mooladeva, once he had related all the events to him. 'How can I remain a woman now that the minister's son is returning? If he discovers that I'm a man, our secret will be out and we'll both be in trouble with the raja.'

Mooladeva sat thinking for a while and then said with a smile, 'I have a plan.' Putting the mantra ball back in Manasvi's mouth, he said, 'Go back to the chief minister's house and wait for me to summon you.'

Then he made another mantra ball and placed that in his friend Shashi's mouth and transformed him into a young man of about twenty years. Finally, he changed himself into the old brahmin again and, accompanied by Shashi, went to the palace to request an audience with the king.

When Raja Munivichara saw the old brahmin alive and well, his heart sank. Nevertheless, he welcomed him warmly and enquired about his well-being.

'Through the grace of the gods, I'm well, now that I've found my son,' Mooladeva replied. 'This is my son,' he said, presenting Shashi to the king.

'I didn't hear from you for a long time. Forgive me but I thought you had perished,' the king said. 'Hence, I was worried that the young woman you left with me would have no one to take care of her, so I married her to my chief minister's son.'

'What adharma is this?' said the old man, jumping to his feet in outrage. 'O King, how dare you give away my son's wife to another? I'll curse you for this sin.'

Hurriedly descending from the throne, Munivichara fell at the brahmin's feet. 'Forgive me, O holy man. Please don't curse me. Tell me, is there anything I can do to compensate you and your son?'

'Yes, there is,' the brahmin replied. 'My son has lost his bride. You must compensate him for his loss. Marry your daughter to my son.'

And so, Raja Munivichara married his daughter to the brahmin Shashi in a Vedic ceremony, in which all the prescribed rituals were performed.

When Manasvi found out that Mooladeva had married his friend Shashi to the princess, he came running to Mooladeva's house. 'How dare you?' he shouted at Shashi. 'That is my wife. Give her back to me.'

'No, she's not. She's my wife,' Shashi declared.

'But she's carrying my child.'

'But I'm the one who married her with full Vedic rituals, with fire as witness.'

'She doesn't love you; she loves me. Give her back to me.'

'She's my wife. I'll never give her to you.'

'She's mine!'

'No. She's mine!'

And the two kept on fighting.

'O King,' said the vetala to Raja Vikramaditya, 'what do you think? Whose wife is the princess—Shashi's or Manasvi's?'

'No doubt she is Shashi's wife,' Vikramaditya replied.

'How have you come to that conclusion? What about the man whose child she is carrying?'

'That child was conceived in secrecy. No one knew they were married. Whereas, Shashi married her in everyone's presence and with full rituals. Therefore, she is Shashi's wife.'

After hearing this response, the vetala took flight, and the corpse returned to the shisham tree.

Tale Fifteen

Who Is More Virtuous in Jimutavahana's Story?

'Are you not tired of this task?' the vetala asked Raja Vikramaditya, as he lifted the corpse and threw it over his shoulder again.

Without a word, Vikramaditya began walking north, in the direction of the bargad tree.

'You've impressed me with your determination. That's why I want to tell you another story. Listen!'

Even higher than pride is the most eminent of mountains—the Himalaya. On its very tip, sitting like a constellation of sun's rays, is Kanchanapuri, the land of vidyadharas. Once, the king of vidyadharas was Jimutaketu, whose glory rivalled that of Indra. Rule of law prevailed in his kingdom, and everyone lived in harmony, free of greed and hate. There was no threat of invading armies, or of robbers and thieves. The earth was green, the fruit trees were bountiful, and cows yielded ample milk. All was well, except that Jimutaketu had no children. Therefore, worshipping the ancestral, wish-fulfilling kalpavriksha in his garden every day, he asked the tree to bestow a son on him. Finally, one day, the kalpavriksha granted his request and declared, 'O King, I am pleased with your devotion. You will have a son who will be valiant and generous and full of compassion for all beings.'

Ten months later, the queen gave birth to a boy, and they named him Jimutavahana, the Rider of Clouds. As the boy began to grow, so did his quality of compassion and his spirit of generosity. One day, the young Jimutavahana said to his father, 'Everything in this world is impermanent and perishable. The only thing of permanence is dharma. If dharma can be gained from charity, then what's the value of wealth? Wealth is as quixotic as lightning. It's also corrupting; it not only corrupts one's self but also other people. That's why I feel that only if we use our wish-fulfilling tree for charity will it serve its rightful purpose. Father, with your permission, I would like to request this tree to make all who are destitute, wealthy.'

Jimutaketu was very pleased with his son's benefactory words, and he agreed without hesitation. Jimutavahana then went to the kalpavriksha and said to it, 'O divine being, please make this earth devoid of poverty. I give you to the poor.'

The tree began to shower gold on earth like rain. There was such an abundance of it that people began to fill their homes with it. At first, all the people were happy and no one remained destitute. However, having an endless supply of gold without toiling for it soon made everyone lazy, greedy, and quarrelsome. Even the officials of the kingdom became careless about their duties; hence, the administration began to weaken. Not surprisingly, the king's relatives, who were on the lookout for just such an opportunity, banded together and mounted an attack on Kanchanapuri. Watching the enemy advance, Jimutavahana said to his father, 'There is no doubt that if you and I fight our relatives in the battlefield, we'll defeat them in no time. However, I don't wish to fight. Just as this body is like a bubble of water, so is kingly wealth like a small lamp in a storm. Which wise person will battle for such impermanence? That's why, dear Father, I have no wish to fight with our relatives. Instead, I'd like to leave this kingdom and go and live in some forest. Let these poor, ignorant relatives enjoy the kingdom.'

'This kingdom is your inheritance. I was taking care of it for you, hoping to one day pass it on to you,' Jimutaketu said to his son. 'If you don't wish to rule it, why should I remain its caretaker? I, too, will give up all this and go with you to live in peace wherever you decide to go.'

Hence, Jimutavahana left Kanchanapuri with his parents and went to Malaya Mountain, where he built an ashram for them and began to take care of them. Here, he also made some friends. One of them was the son of King Malayaketu. His name was Mitravasu, and he was practising to be a siddha—a being who is intellectually and spiritually evolved. Then he met a rishi's son, who was about his own age, and the two became fast friends. One day, as Jimutavahana and the rishi's son were wandering on the mountain, they came upon a Bhagvati temple from which sweet strains of a veena, accompanied by a honeyed voice, were emanating. When they entered the temple, they saw a young woman, whose face was like the moon, and whose very presence brightened the sanctorum. Jimutavahana took one look at her and lost his heart. He came home that day, burning with the agony of love, and as soon as the sun rose, he returned to the temple, hoping to see her again. The young woman was there, but this time, she was with her friends, who were all worshiping the goddess.

'Who is she?' Jimutavahana asked one of her friends.

'She's the daughter of King Malayaketu; her name is Malayavati. And who are you, handsome man?'

'My father is Jimutaketu, and I'm his son, Jimutavahana. My father used to be the king of vidyadharas, but we lost our kingdom to usurping relatives and have come to Malaya Mountain to live peacefully. I have fallen in love with your princess. Please convey this to her.'

When Malayavati received this message from her friends,

she was so flustered that she quickly left the temple and returned home. She spent that whole day in an agitated state, unable to eat, drink, or sleep. Noticing her condition, her attendants informed the queen. The queen then went to her husband and reprimanded him: 'Your daughter has come of age, but you're oblivious to this fact. You should be out looking for a suitable husband for her.'

'You're right, wife,' Malayaketu said and summoned his son, Mitravasu, to assign him the task of finding a groom for Malayavati.

'I already know someone who is very suitable,' Mitravasu told his parents. 'The king of vidyadharas, Jimutaketu, and his son, Jimutavahana, are living on Malaya Mountain. I have met the son and I know he'll make a good husband for my sister.'

Malayaketu was very pleased to hear this and told his son to begin marriage negotiations. Soon, Jimutavahana and Malayavati were married, and after the nuptials, Malayavati came to live with her husband and parents-in-law in the ashram that Jimutavahana had built.

One day, Jimutavahana was roaming on the mountain with his friend and brother-in-law, Mitravasu, when he saw a mound of tiny white bones. 'What is this mound?' he asked Mitravasu.

'These are bones of all the snakes that the divine bird, Garuda, has devoured. Every day, a snake comes out of patala and offers itself to Garuda to be his meal.'

'How has this come to be?'

'Let me tell you the story,' Mitravasu said.

'In the olden days, Rishi Kashyapa married two sisters, Kadru and Vinata. Kadru became the mother of snakes and Vinata, the mother of Garuda. Once, the two placed a wager about the colour of the divine horse, Uchchaihshravas. Kadru said he was black, and Vinata said he was white. The loser was to serve as the winner's slave for 500 years. To defeat her sister and win the bet, Kadru forced her snake sons to help her deceive Vinata by winding themselves in his white tail so he would appear black. When Garuda discovered the trickery, he began to destroy the snakes. He would go to patala whenever he wished and devour hundreds of snakes. Consequently, the snakes began to live in abject fear. Unable to bear this daily carnage of his kin, Vasuki, the king of snakes, went to Garuda and made a pact with him. "If you continue to kill and eat the snakes indiscriminately, you'll be doing yourself a disservice, because soon, there'll be none left," he said. "Instead of attacking the snakes in their home in patala and spreading terror, why don't you stay on the mountain, and we ourselves will send you a snake every day." Garuda agreed to this. From that day on, the snakes have been sending one of their clan to Garuda every day, and he, sitting on a plateau of the mountain, has been devouring them one by one.'

As Mitravasu was telling the story, a young man came running towards them in a rush. Following him was an old woman, wailing, 'Oh Son! Oh Son! My only child. You are my only support in the world. How will I live without you?'

Jimutavahana stopped the man and asked him who he was and why his mother was crying for him.

'My name is Shankhachuda,' said the young man. 'My mother is crying for me because today it's my turn to go to Garuda.'

Jimutavahana then went to the grieving mother and said to her, 'Mother, wipe your tears. I'll save your son. Today, I'll go to Garuda instead of your son.'

'O great soul,' Shankhachuda pleaded with Jimutavahana, 'don't say that. It's not right to hurt the pearl for a mere piece of glass. I'm but an ordinary being; beings like me are born in the world all the time. You, on the other hand, are a true dharma soul. Beings like you are rarely born. If I let you take my place, it'll be a stain on my clan and I don't want to be the one to cause that stain.'

Saying this, that gentle snake Shankhachuda went to the ocean to perform his final worship of Shiva Gokarna. Meanwhile, the compassion-filled Jimutavahana sent his friend Mitravasu away on some pretext. Then he climbed the mountain to the plateau, where Garuda had just landed, causing the earth to tremble with the flapping of his immense wings that shadowed the whole sky. As soon as Jimutavahana came face to face with Garuda, the bird pierced his neck with his beak, and snatching up his bleeding and limp body, flew to the mountaintop to devour him. By this time, Shankhachuda had also arrived on the plateau. Seeing it covered with blood, he realized what had happened. 'I must find Garuda. I must save that great soul, if I still can,' he said, and urgently began climbing to the top.

Just then, Garuda happened to glance at his prey, and he realized that his victim was not a snake but another kind of being. Moreover, not only was he still alive, but he was also smiling. Surprised to see the bliss on his bloody face, Garuda stopped tearing his flesh.

'O king of birds,' Jimutavahana said, 'why have you stopped eating? My body still has flesh and blood left.'

Astonished to hear him say this, Garuda asked him who he was. 'You are not a snake,' he said, 'then why are you here?'

'I *am* a snake. You should keep eating me. Finish what you've started.'

By this time, Shankhachuda had managed to climb to the top, and, seeing Jimutavahana's half eaten body between Garuda's claws, he shouted from afar, 'O Garuda, stop eating him. Stop. He's not a snake. I'm your prey—your meal for today. How did you mistake him for a snake? Release him.'

Garuda staggered in shock and fell off his perch. Then, using his mental power, he looked into the identity of the being he had been devouring and discovered that he was the son of the king of vidyadharas. 'Oh, what a great sin I've committed in pursuit of my cruel desire for revenge,' he said to himself, filled with deep regret. Then he asked Jimutavahana, 'O praiseworthy, high-souled being, why are you sacrificing yourself? Your meritorious actions have put me to shame. In my ignorance, I've lowered the standard of the world's morality.'

'Listen, O divine bird,' Jimutavahana then said to him, 'trees make shade for others, while they themselves scorch in the sun. The more that sandalwood is rubbed, the more its fragrance spreads. The more that sugarcane is cut and stripped, the sweeter it tastes. The more that gold is melted, the more malleable it becomes. Dumb beasts also know how to feed themselves; he who lives for others truly lives and is worthy of praise. He who doesn't use his body and mind to serve others and only serves himself is a wretched fool.'

'O wise man, you've made me realize the grave sins I've been committing,' Garuda said with tears in his eyes. 'I need to repent. What should I do?'

'O King of Birds, why are you sad? If you are truly regretful, then stop eating the snakes this very day and repent for the snakes that you've already killed. This is your penance.'

Just then, Malayavati, who had been looking for her husband, climbed up on the plateau. Seeing Jimutavahana's bloodied body lying on the rock, she fell down in a faint, and when she gained consciousness, she took Jimutavahana's head in her lap and began wailing and lamenting.

'O Princess and glorious wife of this high-souled being,

I'm to blame for your husband's ravaged state,' Garuda said to her. 'But I promise that I'll restore his body to its former self. Please stop crying and forgive me for the grave sin I've committed.' Then, taking flight, Garuda dived into the ocean and scooping amrita in his beak from the ocean floor, returned to the Malaya Mountain. When he sprinkled a few drops of elixir on Jimutavahana's mutilated body, he instantly arose, hale and hearty, with not a scratch on him. Bowing before him, Garuda said, 'O great soul, you have suffered a great deal on my account. Please ask for a boon.'

'Restore the life of all the snakes that you've killed,' Jimutavahana said.

'It shall be done,' Garuda promised and flew off to bring more amrita from the ocean. This time, when he returned, he sprinkled the elixir on the mounds of snake bones, and, instantly, the snakes came back to life. Wiggling and slithering and untangling themselves from each other, they glided across the plateau and descended to patala, where they reunited with their families.

'Raja, here is my question,' the vetala said to Vikramaditya after finishing the story. 'Who do you think is more noble and high-minded—Jimutavahana or Shankachuda, the snake?'

'Shankachuda!' Vikramaditya replied.

'How is that?' the vetala asked. 'Didn't Jimutavahana selflessly offer himself to be devoured in place of the snake? Doesn't that make him more virtuous?'

'It certainly makes him virtuous but not more than the snake. Jimutavahana inculcated and practised magnanimity all his life; whereas, the snake was an ordinary being. He was freed from death and he could have returned to patala to carry on with his life. But he did not; instead, he ran to his devourer to stop him from eating Jimutavahana, who was giving up his life for his sake. Ultimately, Shankachuda proved to be nobler than the noble soul Jimutavahana.'

At this response, the body on Vikramaditya's shoulder shook with ghoulish mirth. Then it flew off and hung itself in the shisham tree.

Tale Sixteen

Who Is Most Virtuous in Unmadini's Story?

As soon as Vikramaditya started back toward the bargad tree, carrying the corpse, the vetala on his shoulder said, 'O Raja, the distance to your destination is long and the night is dark. Let me tell you this great tale to pass the time.'

There was once a king, Raja Devasena, who was the wisest of the wise. In his capital, Shravasti, lived a wealthy moneylender, Ratnadatta, who had a very beautiful daughter. She was famous as Unmadini—one who intoxicates—because whoever saw her became intoxicated with her beauty. When it was time for the girl to be married, the moneylender thought it would be best to offer her to the king first, before he went looking for another groom. Therefore, requesting an audience with Devasena, he said to him, 'Maharaj, I have a daughter who is as precious as a jewel. Please accept her as your bride.'

The king sent his royal brahmins to determine if the girl had all the appropriate marks of beauty that are noted in a woman and that would make her a suitable bride for a king. When the brahmins saw Unmadini, they were rendered speechless. She was not just beautiful; she was the epitome of beauty, with all the marks that define it: wide, innocent, doe eyes; a long, black braid of hair, like a glistening serpent; a sparrow-beak pert nose; eyebrows curved and sharp like strung bows; teeth, a string of pearls; petal-like lips the colour of coral; a long and delicate neck, like a swan's; slim and supple waist, like a tiger's; long limbs, like lotus stalks; buttocks, perfect globes; smooth thighs and tapering legs; finely arched feet with toe-nails the colour of roses topped with half-moons; complexion of champa flowers; and a kokila bird's voice. In other words, her physical appearance was so perfect that it could send Indra's apsaras into hiding.

After seeing her, the brahmins conferred among themselves, and they all agreed that if the king married her, he would surely become addicted to her and lose all interest in the affairs of the kingdom. Therefore, thinking it would be prudent not to tell him the truth, they informed the king that the girl's characteristics were questionable and did not befit a raja of his stature.

Believing his brahmins' assessment, Devasena rejected Ratnadatta's offer. The moneylender felt so insulted by the king's refusal that he hurriedly found another match for his daughter—the king's senapati, Balabhadra—and married Unmadini to him.

One day, touring the capital on his elephant, Devasena saw a woman of such magnificence standing in the terrace of her house, that he almost fell off his mount. Desire coursed through his body like an affliction, and from that moment on, he began to suffer day and night.

'What's the matter, Maharaj?' his personal attendant could not help but ask him. 'I see you suffering, but I see no physical ailment.'

At first, Devasena waved him away, saying, 'It's nothing,' but when the attendant insisted, he told him, 'On my last tour of the city, I saw a woman so beautiful, I don't know whether she's a goddess, apsara, or vidyadhari descended on earth. I only know that I can't forget her. Day and night, she's all I think about. Sleep evades me, food tastes like dust in my mouth, moon rays pierce me like needles, and my heart feels like a leaden weight in my chest. You ask me what is ailing me? I don't know. But whatever it is, I know that she's the cure.'

'Where did you see her, Maharaj?' the attendant asked.

'On the terrace of a house,' the king replied and described the house to him.

'That is no celestial woman, Maharaj,' the attendant replied. 'She's very much human. She's the wife of your general, Balabhadra. Her name is Unmadini. Her father is the city's richest moneylender. Don't you remember he brought you her proposal? When you refused it, he married her to Balabhadra.'

The attendant's words sliced through Devasena like a sword and when he recalled the lies his brahmins had told him, rage flowed from the cut. Summoning the brahmins, he demanded to know why they had lied. 'Tell me why you deceived me,' he thundered. 'That woman is not just beautiful; she is the very epitome of beauty.'

'We agree with you, Maharaj. The moneylender's daughter is indeed the epitome of beauty. That is exactly why we lied. We were afraid that her beauty would distract you from the affairs of the kingdom. It was for the sake of the kingdom that we couldn't tell you the truth.'

Devasena exiled the brahmins from his kingdom. However, punishing them did not ease his pain. Thoughts of Unmadini still filled his mind—her unblemished face, as though it was the source of the moon's light; her proud, firm breasts, like two golden, round-bellied water pots; her pelvic girdle garlanded with jewels, as though to worship Kamadeva. The vision he saw on the terrace haunted him. All day and all night, he burned with lust and desire, losing his appetite, his sleep, and his peace of mind. Ultimately, his body could not bear the deprivation any longer and his physical health also began to deteriorate.

The king's condition did not go unnoticed by Senapati Balabhadra and he soon learned that his own wife was responsible for it. Requesting to meet Devasena in his private room, he said to him, 'Maharaj, I'm your servant. Everything I have is yours, including my wife. Please allow me to bring her to you.'

'How dare you make such an offer?' Devasena shouted at Balabhadra. 'If I, the raja of this land, commit the adharma of taking another's man's wife, on what moral ground can I guide my people? With what face will I sit in the chair of justice and pass judgement? By offering me momentary pleasure with your wife, you are thrusting me into an afterlife of hell. Rightness is in seeing another's wife as your mother, and another's wealth as a lump of soil. Why are you forcing me to stray from the rightful path?'

'What if I leave her in a temple? Then she'll not be my wife any more,' Balabhadra suggested.

'Then I'll punish you for the crime of abandoning your wife,' Devasena warned.

Balabhadra could not utter another word after that and left, feeling helpless and guilty.

Devasena continued to suffer from his affliction that was love and after passing its nine stages: delight, desire, obsession, loss of sleep, lack of appetite, lack of interest in life's pleasures, loss of all shame, loss of bodily weight, and bouts of unconsciousness, he reached the tenth and last stage, of death.

Balabhadra was so grieved at the king's passing that he wept all day and still his heart was heavy. Finally, he went to his guru to ask him what he should do.

'To serve your dharma as the king's servant, you should follow your king to serve him in the afterlife as well,' the guru advised.

Therefore, after praying to Surya and cleansing himself by taking a dip in the river, Balabhadra went to Devasena's burning pyre and stepped into the flames. His last words were: 'Maharaj, I am your true servant. May I continue to serve you in the afterlife.'

When Unmadini learned what her husband had done, she rushed to his guru to ask him what she should do.

'To become sati on a husband's pyre is the highest dharma for a wife,' he advised.

Quickly returning home, Unmadini gave away all her wealth to charity. Then, taking a ritual bath, she went to the burning pyre and, circumambulating it, stepped into the flames with these words: 'O Husband, may I be your wife and serve you life after life.'

'So, King, what do you think?' the vetala asked Raja Vikramaditya. 'Out of these three, who do you think is the most virtuous? Devasena, the king; Balabhadra, his senapati; or Unmadini?'

'The king, of course,' Vikramaditya replied.

'But why not Balabhadra, who selflessly gave up his life and was willing to even give up his wife for the king?'

'It was his duty to serve the king; therefore, the only virtue he earned was that he performed his duty. Unmadini, too, burnt herself on her husband's pyre, only to serve her own dharma as a wife. But Devasena was truly virtuous. Even though he suffered grievously from unfulfilled desire for Unmadini, he didn't accept her when she was offered to him, although, as king, it was his right. Instead, he remained fixed on his dharma at the cost of his own life.'

Hearing this answer, the vetala flew the corpse back to the shisham tree and hung it from a high branch.

Tale Seventeen

Why Did Gunakara Fail in His Quest?

Hefting the dead body on his shoulder, Vikramaditya once again began to walk north. All around him ghouls still screeched, smoke from pyres swirled like gusts of dying breath, and the glow from burning bodies dotted the darkness.

'You are a brave man, Raja,' the vetala in the corpse said to him. 'I'll tell you another story to distract you from your toil.'

Shiva created the most glorious city of Ujjayini to express his love for his beloved Parvati. Once, the king of Ujjayini was Mahasena. Among his subjects was a very wealthy, highly educated, and meritorious brahmin called Devasharma, who had a son named Gunakara. Unlike his father, the son had acquired many bad habits, such as gambling. One day, overcome by the urge to gamble, Gunakara went to a gambling den and started playing with high stakes, convinced that luck would favour him. But luck was not on his side that day. Not only did he lose all the money that he was carrying, but he also lost the very clothes he was wearing. However, his gambler's mind was not deterred, and feeling certain that his luck would turn, he began to play on credit. In no time, he lost a lot of money that he did not even have. When the winners discovered that he did not have the coin to pay up, they beat him to an inch of his life and deposited his unconscious, near-naked body beside a well outside the city.

When Gunakara regained his senses, he wondered what he would do. He had no clothes and no money, and he couldn't go home, because he didn't know how he would explain his bruised body and swollen face to his parents. Finally, coming to his feet with great difficulty, he began to look for shelter and found an abandoned Shiva temple near the well. He spent the night there, shivering in the cold, groaning in pain, and ignoring the hunger gnawing at his stomach. As soon as dawn broke, he went looking for food and clothing and came upon a sanyasi. He was sitting cross-legged, eyes closed in meditation and right arm resting on a trishool planted in the dirt beside him. Bowing to him, Gunakara sat down near him without a word. The sanyasi opened his eyes and asked him if he wished to eat.

'Yes,' Gunakara said. 'If you give me food, I'll eat it.'

Reaching into his sack, the sanyasi brought out a skull bowl filled with food and offered it to him.

'I'm a brahmin,' Gunakara said. 'How can I eat from this skull?'

The sanyasi then chanted a mantra and instantly, a beautiful yakshini appeared before them. She bowed to the sanyasi with folded hands and said, 'Command me, O yogi. What should I do?'

'This man is my guest,' the sanyasi replied. 'Take care of him.'

That very instant, Gunakara found himself in a golden palace filled with beautiful maidens hurrying to and fro. Several of them ushered him into a washroom, where they bathed him with fragrant soaps and oil and dressed him in silk garments. Then they brought him to a hall and seated him before a lavish spread of food. After he had had his fill, one of the women placed a paan in his mouth and some others began to sing and dance to entertain him. When night fell, two women took him by the hands and led him to a well-furnished bedroom, where they helped him undress and then made love to him until he was satiated. When his eyes became heavy with sleep, they covered him with a silk coverlet and tiptoed out of the room.

In the morning, when Gunakara opened his eyes, he was lying on the cold, hard ground near the Shiva temple. The yakshini, the gold palace, the beautiful women, and the soft bed with silk sheets were all gone. But the sanyasi was still there, sitting exactly as he had been when Gunakara had first found him, with his eyes closed and his arm resting on a trishool. 'Swami,' Gunakara said, sitting up, 'where is that celestial beauty who took care of me last night? How did you summon her? Can you please teach me how to summon her?'

The sanyasi laughed. 'This is a tantric vidya, and it can only be acquired with arduous discipline. It's not something any ordinary man can achieve.'

'If you teach it to me, I promise that I'll prove to be an ideal pupil.'

'Fine,' said the sanyasi. 'I'll teach it to you. Come with me to the river. It has to be learned in the water.' The sanyasi then took Gunakara to the riverbank and, teaching him a mantra, told him to go and stand in the water, shoulder-deep. 'Stay there for forty days,' he instructed. 'And continuously repeat the mantra. Don't move, or sit, or leave the water,' he warned. 'When forty days have passed, come to the shore, and you'll find me there, seated beside a fire. Step into this fire and allow yourself to burn in it. When you emerge from it, you'll possess the knowledge you seek.'

Following the sanyasi's instructions, Gunakara walked into the river till the water was up to his shoulders and began to chant the mantra over and over. After just a few hours, his feet began to feel numb and his body became fatigued. However, he stayed where he was and kept repeating the mantra. When night fell and darkness crept over the water, his mind began to play tricks on him, conjuring up all kinds of horrors of giant fish swallowing him. Somehow, he managed to rein in his wayward thoughts and focus on the mantra. The next day, the sun shone brightly and his body was scorched; yet, he was able to ignore the discomfort and continue. That night the fish that came to swallow him were larger and more ferocious, so he chanted the mantra more loudly. In this way, for forty days, he was able to remain in one spot, with his mind focused on the words he uttered repeatedly. On the forty-first morning, he opened his eyes and waded to the shore. The sanyasi was there, sitting beside a fire, just as he had said he would be. Excited at the prospect of concluding his quest, Gunakara hurriedly went to meet him. Just then, a group of people came rushing towards him, calling his name. When he looked at their faces, he realized they were his family, who had somehow found him. 'Where were you?' his mother cried, putting her arms around him. 'Your father searched for you everywhere. We were so worried,' she cried. His father then embraced him and kissed him on the forehead. 'Come home,' he said. 'I'm an old man, and I need my son. Why have you abandoned us? Don't you know that forsaking your parents is a sin? Don't you know that parents are worthy of worship—more revered than any pilgrimage? Besides, this is your age to become a householder. All men must fulfil this dharma. What are you doing in the company of sanyasis?' Gunakara was soon surrounded by all his relatives, and all of them urged him to return home.

'I should go home,' he said to himself. 'My old parents need me. Who else do they have to support them in their old age? I must do it.' But then he thought: who is my father? Who is my mother? Who are these relatives? A person is reborn many times, and, in each birth, he acquires many relationships. Who am I but a mixture of semen and blood? I'll die and be born again and again, assuming a body that is nothing but a vessel full of foul things like urine and excrement. Let me jump into the flames and acquire the yakshini who will let me experience heavenly pleasures. Then his mind asked more questions: but what if I jump into the fire and don't acquire the knowledge? What if it's a real fire, and I actually burn to death? Then I'll lose both my family and the yakshini. No, no, he thought, stopping himself from thinking such thoughts. Let me finish what I've started. If what the sanyasi has promised does occur, and I acquire the yakshini, then I can go to my parents with the ability to give them anything they want. Thinking this, he walked away from his family and stepped into the fire, chanting the mantra.

Flames licked his body, but to his surprise, they were as cold as snow. After he had been in the fire for some time, the flames vanished and he found himself sitting on the ground beside the sanyasi. This is it, he thought, I've completed the trials. Now it's time to test my vidya. Closing his eyes, he chanted the mantra to summon the yakshini, but nothing happened; she did not appear.

Confused and feeling let down, Gunakara opened his eyes and said to the sanyasi, 'Swami, I followed every instruction you gave me and completed all the steps without faltering, but I can't summon the yakshini.'

'No, you did not do exactly as I instructed. Did you utter the mantra as the fire burned you?'

'But the fire did not burn me swami; it felt as cold as snow.'

'Then you have failed in your quest,' the yogi declared.

'Why did Gunakara fail?' the vetala asked Vikramaditya. 'Why wasn't he able to summon the yakshini? O Raja, tell me the answer, if you know it, and remember that if you don't answer, your head will be scattered all over this cremation ground in a thousand pieces.'

'He was double-minded. That is why he couldn't summon the yakshini. To achieve a goal, one must be single-minded. A divided mind leads to failure. Just effort doesn't achieve success. One can shoot the arrow, but without the focus of one's eye, the arrow doesn't know the target.'

'Why do you say he wasn't single-minded? Did he not remain in the water for forty days, repeating the mantra? Did he not jump into the flames as the sanyasi had told him to do? And he did all this with the single goal of acquiring the knowledge to summon the yakshini.'

'It is true that he followed the sanyasi's instructions, but in the midst of his pursuit, he was conflicted and considered returning to his family. To acquire something single-minded, unfaltering pursuit is requisite.'

The vetala in the dead body squealed with laughter, and the corpse flew back to the shisham tree. Raja Vikramaditya, too, turned around and began walking briskly in the same direction.

Tale Eighteen

Who Is Haridatta's Real Father?

'O King, I feel for you. Trudging back and forth between the shisham tree and the bargad tree, carrying this heavy body, you must be exhausted,' the vetala said to Vikramaditya, as soon as he started back to where the yogi was waiting. 'Here's another story to entertain you while you attempt to deliver this corpse to that tantric.'

There was a city, Kubalapura, which was as magnificent as Indra's Amravati, and in it lived Raja Sudakshina, who was as glorious as Indra. In his kingdom, people shed tears only when their eyes were stung with smoke and for no other reason. Everyone everywhere talked about love, never about hate, crime, or killing. Although the security guards that guarded that city were equipped with punishing rods, no one ever got punished, because no one ever committed an act that required punishment. It was, indeed, a happy and prosperous land. In this land lived a very wealthy businessman, named Dhanakshi, whose daughter, Dhanavati, was as beautiful as an apsara in Indra's heaven. Dhanakshi married his young daughter to another businessman, Gauridanta, and some years later, the couple had a daughter whom they named Mohini.

It so happened that just after Mohini's first birthday, her father, Gauridanta passed away. Since he did not leave a male heir, his relatives claimed his wealth and property, and they threw Dhanavati out. Thus, one dark and stormy night, Dhanavati found herself on the road, homeless and destitute, carrying her infant daughter in her arms, looking for shelter. Somehow, she ended up in the cremation ground. As she stumbled around, peering into the darkness, trying to find a place to spend the night, her shoulder hit the foot of a man who was hanging from a cross.

'Ahhhh,' the man cried out in pain. 'Who is causing me such pain at this time when I am awaiting death?'

'Oh! Forgive me,' Dhanavati said, 'I didn't see you. It was an accident. I didn't mean to cause you pain.'

'Pain and pleasure, sadness and joy—no one can give these to someone else. These are written in a person's fate, even before he is born, and he has no choice but to experience them in his life. Anyone who makes claims such as "I've done this," is an ignorant fool. The lives of people are tied to the thread of fate, and wherever that thread pulls them, they must go. No one knows the ways of fate. We may plan something, but something else may happen. Where it'll happen, when it'll happen—only fate knows, and a person will somehow find himself driven by circumstance to that very spot, at that precise moment.'

'Who are you? And why are you hanging from this cross?' Dhanavati asked.

'I'm a thief, and this cross is my punishment for robbing people. But look at my fate: I've been nailed to this cross for three days, yet death evades me.'

'Why is that?' Dhanavati asked.

'It's because I'm unmarried and don't have any children. For salvation, one needs offspring, or it's an offence against creation.' The man was silent for moment, and then he said, 'You can help me. Give me your daughter in marriage. In exchange, I'll give you one thousand gold coins.'

'But you're on a cross, close to death, and my daughter is just one year old.'

'When your daughter comes of age, find a young brahmin for her and give him five hundred of the gold coins. The sons she bears from that man will be in my name, and they'll be my salvation.'

It is said that the root of evil is desire, and the root of sorrow is attachment. Desiring the gold that the thief promised, Dhanavati agreed to his proposition. Holding her daughter, she circumambulated the cross on which he was hanging, four times, as is the custom in wedding ceremonies. And, thus, the dying thief and the infant girl Mohini were married.

After the ritual of marriage, the thief instructed Dhanavati to go east. 'You'll soon come to a well with a bargad tree beside it. Dig near the roots of that tree and you'll find a pot of gold coins. Take it; it's yours.' Saying this, the thief finally breathed his last.

Walking eastward, Dhanavati soon came to a well beside a large bargad tree. Laying her infant down, she dug near the roots of the tree and found the buried pot of gold. Then she sat down with her infant in her arms and rested under the tree for the night. As soon as the sun rose, she walked to the adjoining town, where her parents lived, and told them everything that had happened to her, including her encounter with the thief. Then, with her father's help, she cremated the thief and had his ashes sprinkled in four pilgrimage sites. After that, she returned to Kubalapura and, using some of the gold from the pot, had a mansion built for herself and her daughter.

Mohini grew up to be a beautiful and accomplished young woman. One day, she was standing in the terrace with her friends, when she saw a very handsome young brahmin walking in the street below. She instantly lost her heart to him and sent one of her friends to invite him to her house to meet her mother.

The young brahmin's name was Manaswami. He was on his way to conclude a business deal but, intrigued by the invitation that Mohini's friend brought, he came into the house to meet Dhanavati. As soon as Dhanavati saw Manaswami, she was reminded of her promise to the thief. Seating the young man across from her, she said to him, 'Son, I have a proposition for you. My daughter is young and beautiful. If you stay here with her, I'll give you five hundred gold coins.'

The brahmin youth had little time to spare, but the idea of five hundred gold coins was too enticing.

'I accept,' he said to Dhanavati, 'but I can only stay one night.'

'That should be ample,' Dhanavati replied and called her maids to take care of the guest.

Manaswami was given the eight honours befitting an honoured guest: fragrance, new clothes, ornaments, music, delicious food, paan and betel nuts, a comfortable bed, and beautiful women. Once he was suitably guested, he and Mohini had a quick nuptial ceremony and, following that, he was taken to the bedroom, where Mohini was waiting for him. All it took was an exchange of one fervent look, and the young couple fell into each other's arms, their bodies aflame. The next day, when Mohini's friends asked her to share the details of her union with her husband, this is how she described it:

'When he sat down beside me, my heart was pounding,' she told them. 'When he reached for my hand, my whole body began to tremble. Then my jewelled belt became untied by itself, and my garments began to slip off. When he clasped me to his breast, I melted into him and lost all my senses. I can't recount anything after that, because I have no recollection of it. All I can say is that it's true what people say about men who are renowned, brave, smart, talented, and protective. They can never be forgotten—not even after they've left.'

Manaswami left that morning, but Mohini was already with child and in due time, she gave birth to a son. One night, after her baby was born, she saw a yogi in her dream. His hair was matted and his body was covered with ashes. There was a crescent moon on his forehead, and he was sitting on a thousand-petalled lotus. White snakes wound around his middle and ranged around his neck. He was wearing a garland of skulls and holding a begging bowl in one hand and a trishool in the other. His countenance was quite terrifying. Mohini watched him go to her mother and say to her, 'Tomorrow night put a thousand gold coins in a basket, along with the boy, and place it outside the gate of the king's palace.'

Mohini woke up and ran to her mother to relate the dream. When Dhanavati heard her daughter's dream, she knew the time had come for her to fulfil her promise. Taking the infant boy from her daughter's arms, she placed him in a basket and filled it with gold coins. Then she went to the king's palace and left the basket outside the gate.

That night, the king too had a dream in which he saw a yogi with ten arms, five heads, and three eyes—the third one in the centre of his forehead. There was a crescent moon in the coil of his matted hair and he was holding a sharp trishool in one of his hands. He was so frightening to look at that the king started trembling in fear. 'O Raja, there is a basket at your gate,' the yogi said to the king. 'The boy in that basket will be your successor.'

The king woke up with the yogi's words still loud and clear in his head. Quickly summoning his man, he said to him, 'There is a basket lying at the main gate. Go and fetch it right away.'

When the basket was brought to him, he opened it to find a newborn boy in it, along with a thousand gold coins.

He was very happy to see the newborn and even happier to see the gold.

The next morning, the king summoned his priests and astrologers and asked them to identify marks of excellence on the boy. 'Maharaj,' said one of the brahmins, 'an ideal man has thirty-two marks. Three of these are already visible in the boy, even though he's only an infant: his chest is broad, his body is long, and his face is fair and wide.'

The king removed a pearl necklace that he was wearing and placed it around the brahmin's neck. 'I'm grateful to you for pointing out these marks,' he said. 'Can you see any other marks of excellence?'

'A deep navel, deep voice, and deep breath, broad thighs, and a broad forehead are all marks of an ideal male,' another brahmin replied. 'In addition, prominent shoulders, chin, and nose, and short and shapely fingernails are also counted as marks of excellence in a male. A ruddy complexion and ruddiness in the corners of the eyes, inside of lips and nails, on the palms and the soles of the feet are all signs of good health. Among signs of nobility are long arms, strong jaw and nose, and a wide space between the eyebrows. Maharaj, all these signs indicate a man who will rule the earth. This boy is already showing signs of excellence and we have no doubt that by the time he comes of age, he'll possess all thirty-two marks.'

Thanking the brahmins and astrologers, the king placed the boy in the queen's lap so that he could be officially adopted. Then a horoscope was drawn up and the boy was named Haridatta. Great celebrations followed, and all the citizens of the kingdom came to see the crown prince and congratulate the king and queen.

Haridatta was a handsome and brilliant boy. By the time he was sixteen years old, he had completed his study of the nine shastras and training in fourteen accomplishments. At such a young age, he already had several marks of excellence and nobility. Watching him grow, the king felt grateful and content, knowing that his kingdom would be in good hands after he passed.

Some years later, in some city far away, the young brahmin who had fathered Haridatta died. And soon after, the old king and queen who adopted him also passed away.

Haridatta ascended to the throne and proved to be an able ruler. One day, thinking about his parents, he felt the urge to pilgrimage to Gaya and make sacrifices so that his ancestors could reap the benefits in their afterlife. Arriving at the sacred Phalgu River, Haridatta sat on its bank and made pindas—ritual balls of cooked rice—in the name of his father. However, when he offered the pindas in the river, three hands emerged from the water to receive the balls. Haridatta was nonplussed. He didn't know in which hand to place the pindas.

The vetala stopped telling the story and said to Raja Vikramaditya, 'You see, King, the three hands belonged to the three men who could claim to be Haridatta's father. But he can't have three fathers. Who do you think is Haridatta's rightful father? Who deserves the ritual pindas—the thief to whom his mother promised deliverance, the young brahmin who fathered him, or the old king who adopted him?'

'The thief,' declared Raja Vikramaditya.

'Why not the young brahmin who fathered him? And why not the old king who adopted him and brought him up with the love of a father?'

'The brahmin's sperm was purchased for five hundred gold coins and the king cared for him in exchange for one thousand gold coins. How could they deserve the pinda of a father?

Only the thief was deserving. It was in his name that Mohini birthed the boy.'

As soon as the vetala heard the answer, he flew back to the shisham tree.

Tale Nineteen

Why Did the Boy Laugh on Being Put to Death?

This time, when Vikramaditya returned to the shisham tree, he was astonished to see that instead of a single corpse, there were many dead bodies hanging from its branches. What is this trickery, he thought. This must be the vetala's illusion. But how am I to know which corpse is real? Trying to pick the real one from the illusory may take me all night and I only have till dawn to deliver the body to the yogi, or I'll have broken my word to him. And if that happens, I'll have no choice but to commit my body to fire.

Hearing the raja's inner dialogue, the vetala was impressed by his integrity and sense of honour. In an instant, he removed the illusion, and Vikramaditya was relieved to see all the bodies except one disappear. Quickly, he cut it down and settling it on his shoulder again, began to walk to the bargad.

'So, King, are you ready for the next story?' the vetala asked. 'Listen!'

There is a city called Chitrakoot. Once, a king called Roopadatta lived there. He was very fond of hunting and often went to the forest to shoot deer. During one hunt, he got separated from his retinue and searching for his men, came upon a lake that was like a setting for Kamadeva's sweet schemes. Pink and red lotuses floated in the clear, blue water, and blossoming trees lined its sides. Varied birds twittered all around and the air was fragrant with the scent of flowers.

Dismounting and tethering his horse, Roopadatta sat down near the lake to rest.

It so happened that this idyllic site was part of Maharishi Kanava's ashram, and his daughter, Indivaraprabha, often came here to pick flowers. On this day, too, soon after Roopadatta arrived, Indivaraprabha came to the lake, her ankle bells tinkling, her hips swaying, and her long, black, silken curls cascading down her back. Roopadatta watched her as she plucked flowers and collected them in her dupatta. He had never seen anyone as lovely as her and was smitten. When she turned to leave, he said softly, 'O beautiful maiden, what manner of conduct is this?'

Indivaraprabha swung around. She had not seen Roopadatta sitting in the shade of a tree.

'I've come as a guest to your ashram,' Roopadatta continued, 'and you've not taken care of me. People say that even if a low-caste person arrives as a guest at the house of a high-caste person, he must be treated with honour and respect. Not just a person of low caste; even if a thief, or an enemy, or a deceiver comes to your house, he must be treated like a guest. They say a guest is as revered as a guru. Yet here I am, still waiting for your attention.'

Gazing at the handsome man, Indivaraprabha lost herself in his eyes, just as Roopadatta was captivated by the loveliness of her face. Thus, oblivious to the world around them, neither one of them noticed when Rishi Kanava came and stood beside them. 'Who are you and what are you doing in this forest?' the rishi asked the king.

Roopadatta quickly stood up and bowed. 'I am Raja Roopadatta,' he replied. 'I came to this forest to hunt.'

'Why do you indulge in such adharma? It's a practice in which many suffer the consequences of man's evil actions. Are you not concerned about the impact such adharma will have on your life and afterlife?'

'O wise rishi, please tell me about dharma and adharma. I truly want to know.'

'It is adharma to kill forest-dwelling creatures who are free and live on food and water that the forest provides; they're not anyone's property. On the other hand, it's considered high dharma to protect animals, birds, and humans. Those who bestow fearlessness on the fearful gain the merits of the greatest act of charity. It is said, O Raja, that no penance is greater than forgiveness, no happiness is greater than contentment, no wealth is greater than friendship, and no dharma is greater than compassion. Those who fulfil their dharma with diligence, without the egoity of wealth, talent, education, fame, and glory, enjoy final liberation. Also on the path of dharma are those who are truthful, content, and respectful of their wives, whereas those who mistreat the poor, helpless, and renunciants incur great adharma. And, know this, if a king remains immersed only in his own pleasure and ignores his kingly duties, he goes straight to hell. Naraka also awaits that man who has sexual relations with his friend's wife or daughter or a woman who is in her eighth or ninth month of pregnancy. These are a few instructions of dharma and adharma from the shastras.'

'O wise rishi, thank you for instructing me about what constitutes dharma and what actions lead one into the evil depths of adharma. This is my resolution: whatever adharmas I've committed in my life due to my ignorance are a thing of my past. From this day onwards, I'll diligently follow only the path of dharma.'

'I'm pleased with your intention,' Rishi Kanava said. 'Ask me for a boon.'

'If you are truly happy with me and want to bestow something on me, then please allow me to marry your daughter.'

Hence, with Rishi Kanava's blessing, Raja Roopadatta married Indivaraprabha. After the nuptials, Roopadatta seated his new bride in front of him on his horse and started for home. When they were about halfway through their journey, the sun set. Thinking it best to stop for the night, Roopadatta found a peepul tree near a water spring and made a makeshift bed of soft leaves under it, spreading his own silk shawl over the leaves. Then, tending to his horse and washing himself at the spring, he lay down next to his bride and made love to her. Soon, lulled by their satiated desire and the gentle rippling of the water, they both drifted off to sleep.

In the middle of the night, they were suddenly woken up by a voice that thundered above them: 'Who are you? And what are you doing near my tree?' It was Brahmarakshasa Jwalamukha, who had just returned home after finishing his evening meal of human flesh. As tall as the peepul tree, with skin the colour of a dark rain cloud and teeth as white as a snowy mountaintop, he stood beside the sleeping couple, rage sparking in his red eyes.

The king and his bride sat up, trembling in shock and fear. 'I am Raja Roopadatta, and this is my bride,' the king stated.

'This is my peepul tree. I sleep here. You've taken my spot, and to teach you a lesson I'll eat this woman,' the brahmarakshasa roared.

Indivaraprabha scooted behind her husband with a cry, shaking in every limb, and Roopadatta appealed to the brahmarakshasa: 'Please don't do that. I'll give you whatever you want.'

The brahmarakshasa humphed and said, 'Fine. If you cut

off the head of a seven-year-old boy and place it in my hand, I'll spare your bride.'

Roopadatta was horrified to hear his condition, but he had no choice. 'Come to my palace after seven days and I'll give you the head of the seven-year-old boy,' he said.

'I'll see you in seven days,' was the brahmarakshasa's ominous promise before he disappeared.

Roopadatta calmed his terror-stricken wife, and as soon as the sun rose, he rode at breakneck speed back to his palace. Once there, he called his trusted minister and told him about the happenings in the forest and his encounter with the brahmarakshasa. He also told him about the deal he had to make to save his bride. 'What was I to do?' he said in despair to the minister. 'I had to make him that promise. But now I need to kill a seven-year-old boy before he arrives. Who will give me their young son just so I can cut off his head?'

'Maharaj, I have a plan,' the minister said and told him what he was thinking.

Roopadatta nodded his head in approval. 'I think your plan might work,' he said.

The minister had the royal goldsmith make a twenty-five-kilogram boy of pure gold studded with precious gems. Then he had that statue paraded in the streets of the city on a wheeled cart that was guarded by a squad of lance- and shield-bearing soldiers. Alongside that cart, a kettledrum announced to the citizens: 'Is anyone willing to exchange this pure gold statue of a boy for his seven-year-old son, whose head will be cut off?'

For two days, no one came forward to make the exchange. On the third day, an impoverished brahmin, whose body was no more than skin and bones, heard the announcement and rushed home to talk to his wife. 'We have three sons,' he said to her. 'Let's give away one of them for that boy made of gold. We'll sell it, and with the money we make, you and I and our two remaining sons can live comfortably for a long time.'

'My heart breaks to even think about this, but I agree with you,' said the wife. 'However, you can't take our youngest, because I love him the most.'

'And I can't give away our eldest, because I'm most attached to him,' said the brahmin.

'That leaves only me,' said the middle son, who was standing at the door, listening to his parents' conversation. 'O Father, don't hesitate. Take me to the king right away and exchange me for the gold boy.'

'Forgive me, son,' the brahmin said to his boy. 'In this world, only wealth has value. The indigent have no happiness, and their lives have no value.'

And so the poor brahmin led his middle son to the soldiers and exchanged him for the gold statue. The boy was brought to the palace where he was bathed and dressed in fine clothes, fed a sumptuous meal, and given a soft bed with silk sheets. On the seventh day, at daybreak, Jwalamukha the brahmarakshasa appeared in Raja Roopadatta's court. The king was waiting for him. He respectfully offered him a comfortable seat and then called for the boy. When the brahmin's son was brought in, the raja seated him on an asana and ritualized him with sandalwood, incense, flowers, vermillion, paan, and new clothes. Then, telling him to stand, he raised his sword.

The boy began to cry, but even as the sword struck his neck, he laughed.

'O Raja, the boy's crying is understandable, but tell me this—why did he laugh?' the vetala asked Raja Vikramaditya. 'And let me remind you that if you don't give me an answer, your head will become a thousand tiny pieces.'

'I know the answer,' Vikramaditya replied. 'The boy laughed because he realized the callousness of the world. He thought, when you're a child, a mother protects you; when you grow into boyhood, a father takes care of you. The king protects all his subjects, and celestial beings feel compassion for all. But in my case, my mother and father both gave me up for gold, the king is standing over me with a sword ready to cut off my head for his own benefit, and this celestial being is waiting to see me die. No one feels pity for me. If this is the way of the world, what use is crying or lamenting?'

The vetala cackled with laughter and the dead body lifted off Vikramaditya's shoulder yet again and flew back to the shisham tree.

Tale Twenty

Who Loved Most Deeply in This Story of Unfulfilled Love?

Raja Vikramaditya trudged back to the shisham tree again, and climbing up to the hanging corpse, cut it loose. Once again, jumping off the tree and hoisting the dead body on his shoulder, he began walking in the direction of the bargad tree, where the yogi was waiting for him.

'O Raja, it seems that nothing will deter you from your task. I like a man with such single-minded resolve. I think you deserve another story,' the vetala said to him.

Like a replica of Indra's Indrapuri, there is a vast and beautiful city on earth, called Vishala. Once upon a time, it was ruled by the renowned king Padmanabha. In that city also lived a very wealthy businessman named Arthadatta, whose daughter Anangamanjari was more beautiful than Indra's apsaras. When she came of age, Arthadatta married her to the son of another businessman in Tamralipti. However, instead of sending his only daughter to her husband's house, he made his son-in-law, Maniverma, move in with them.

Anangamanjari and Maniverma lived in matrimonial bliss for months. Then, desiring to see his parents, Maniverma went to Tamralipti to visit them. It was the season of summer when he left. The sun's rays struck the earth like torture and dusty heat waves rose to the sky like parched entreaties for rain. In such weather, Anangamanjari walked around her house, wearing only a thin garment and constantly rubbing cool sandal paste on her skin. One day, sitting by a window, she saw the royal priest's handsome young son Kamalakara walking down the street, and such a stab of desire hit her that she gasped. Just then, Kamalakara looked up and saw the thinly clad, moon-like Anangamanjari and was also struck, as though by a shaft of lightning. Staggering from the impact, he somehow managed to get home. Anangamanjari, on the other hand, just sat by the window all day, stupefied. When her friend Malti came to visit her in the evening, she called her name several times but Anangamanjari did not hear her. Malti had to shake her shoulder to get her attention. 'What has happened to you?' she asked with concern.

'O Kamadeva,' Anangamanjari said, 'Lord Shiva burned you to ashes, but still you don't refrain from striking innocent, hapless women with your arrows.'

'What are you saying?' Malti asked, shaking her shoulder again.

'O moon,' said Anangamanjari, 'rising from the ocean, full of the elixir of life, your rays are always smooth, cool strings of pearls; why are you blazing today and burning my skin with your light?'

Malti finally began to understand Anangamanjari's state and chided her. 'Hush!' she said. 'Have you no shame? The chakor bird pines for the moon and suffers in silence. The lotus, pining for sunlight, folds its petals in silence at night. Your sorrow, like them, knows no bounds. I understand that, but you must bear it in silence.'

'The love god has made me shameless. The strike of his arrows is too fresh and too deep for me to remain quiet.'

'What are you saying?' Malti said. 'How have you suddenly been struck with love and desire?'

'Who can resist Kamadeva's five arrows of love? When

they strike, a person becomes helpless.'

'But you have a husband.'

'Yes, and he's far away. He's left me to suffer in the spring of my youth. But what am I to do now? Each breath I draw is painful, and my body is burning up in in this inexplicable fire.'

'You poor thing,' Malti consoled her friend and tried to cool her by spreading more sandalwood paste on her body and placing a garland of cool-petalled lotuses around her neck. 'Have patience,' she said. 'Love's desire ebbs in time.'

After some time, Malti left, wishing her friend solace and promising to return shortly. Anangamanjari lay on her bed for a while, willing the sandal paste and the lotus flowers to cool her, but their sweet fragrance only heightened her desire. Sighing deeply, she got up and went into the garden. There, she made a noose from her dupatta and stringing it from the peepul tree, put it around her neck with a prayer to the goddess to make Kamalakara her husband in her next birth. Just then, Malti came running towards her. 'Stop! Stop!' she cried. 'What are you doing? This is no way to end your pain.'

'Then please tell me how I can end it,' Anangamanjari begged. 'I can't bear it. My heart burns for another man, while my modesty reminds me of my husband.'

'Tell me, who is this man you're pining for?'

'Kamalakara, the royal priest's son,' Anangamanjari stated and then told her friend how they saw each other from the window.

'I promise I'll bring Kamalakara to you. Just wait here, and don't do anything foolish,' Malti said and rushed out of the garden to go to Kamalakara. When she arrived at his house, she discovered that he, too, was in the garden, lying on a cot under a tree, moaning, 'I'm dying! I'm dying!' while his friends tended to him. One of them was waving a banana-leaf fan to cool him and another was washing him with rose water.

'Have patience,' his friends said gently.

'How can I have patience?' he moaned. 'Bring me some poison. Without Anangamanjari, I'll die anyway, but it'll be a long, suffering death. Kill me now. Save me from the torture of a prolonged death. Just give me some poison so that I can end my life.'

Hearing him say this, Malti stepped forward. 'O Kamalakara, come with me right now to Anangamanjari. She's waiting for you. Like you, she, too, is suffering. The moon's light falls on her like the scorching rays of the sun, the gentle southern breeze burns her like a forest fire. The lotus touches her like an ember.'

Kamalakara jumped up and pushed his friends away. 'O kind lady,' he said to Malti, 'your words are like life-giving elixir. Take me to my beloved right away.'

The two of them then hurried to Anangamanjari's garden, where Malti led Kamalakara to the peepul tree under which she had left Anangamanjari. She was still there; however, she was no longer alive. Seeing her lifeless, Kamalakara's heart burst in his chest, and breathing his last, he fell on his beloved's body.

The people of Vishala prepared a single pyre for the lovers. They did not have the heart to separate the two bodies. And that is how they were laid on the pyre—in an embrace.

Just as flame was touched to the pyre, Maniverma, Anangamanjari's husband, arrived there. Wailing, he ran to the pyre and was so overcome with grief that even though he saw his wife's body in another man's embrace, he climbed into the flames and burned to death.

'So, you see, King, all three died of love,' the vetala said to Vikramaditya. 'But, out of the three, who do you think was the most deeply in love?'

'The husband, of course,' Vikramaditya stated. 'Even though he saw his beloved in the arms of another man, he wanted to die with her.'

Hearing the answer, the vetala lifted the corpse from Vikramaditya's shoulder and flew it back to the shisham tree.

Tale Twenty-one

Which Learned Man Is the Bigger Fool?

After Vikramaditya had brought down the dead body and placed it on his shoulder again to deliver it to the yogi, the vetala on his shoulder said to him, 'Here's a tale that'll surely entertain you.'

There is a city called Jaisthala, which used to be ruled by a king called Vardhamana. In that city lived an erudite brahmin, Vishnuswami. He had four sons, but all four were a disappointment to him. The eldest was a gambler, the second spent all his time with prostitutes, the third was a lustful adulterer, and the fourth was a godless atheist.

Vishnuswami often advised his sons to change their ways and gain knowledge, but his words fell on deaf ears. One day, he gathered his sons and tried to counsel them one last time. Addressing the gambler, he warned, 'Lakshmi never stays in the house of a gambler. And, know this: law books prescribe that a gambler's ears and nose should be cut off, and he should be exiled from the land. Also, my son, a gambler's wife and children are always on the brink of homelessness and destitution, because they never know when the gambler may lose everything.'

Then, turning to his second son, Vishnuswami said, 'Those who lose their hearts to prostitutes are never happy, because the nature of a prostitute's livelihood is faithlessness. My son, being with a prostitute means losing all your wealth, because she won't let you go until she has drained you dry. Sensible men know that a woman who wins your heart in a trice does so with guile; therefore, they stay away from such women. It's the ignorant who love them and lose everything—truth, modesty, reputation, logic, family, friends, and dharma.'

After that, he turned to his third son. 'Wise men say that adultery is the root of sorrow,' he told him. 'He who remains seeped in the lustfulness of youth, burns in fires of hell. The woman who accepts advances from an adulterer should herself never be trusted. If she can deceive her husband, how can she be faithful to her lover? How can a tomcat that eats her own young spare the mice? My son, do you know what punishment law books prescribe for adulterers? Their faces are blackened, and they are paraded through the streets, riding backwards on a donkey.'

For the fourth son, Vishnuswami had no advice except his last words, which he addressed to all four of his sons. 'Dear sons,' he said, 'filled with the arrogance of youth, those who fail to acquire knowledge in their younger years, suffer the consequences in their old age. Therefore, listen to your father and educate yourselves before it's too late.'

Vishnuswami's words finally hit the mark and made his sons think. 'We should go and acquire knowledge,' the four of them concurred. 'But for that, one needs a guru,' the youngest brother said. 'I don't think we can find a guru who will agree to teach all four of us.' Hence, they decided that each one would find a guru for himself in a different town, and at the completion of their education, they would meet at a designated spot. Then they all went their separate ways and found gurus and as planned, met up many years later, eager to demonstrate the knowledge they had acquired.

'What did you learn?' they asked each other.

'I can take a pile of animal bones and recreate the structure of the animal to whom the bones belonged,' said the eldest.

'With the science I learned, I can put flesh and blood in this skeleton,' said the second.

'I can give it five senses. I can also give it hair,' said the third.

'And I can put life in it,' said the youngest.

'Why don't we test our knowledge?' said one of the brothers. 'Let's find a heap of bones and demonstrate what we can do.'

And so the four brothers went into the forest, found a heap of bones and carried it to an open spot. Then the eldest arranged the bones and declared that they belonged to a lion. The second son then restored the lion's flesh and blood. The third restored his five senses and his mane. Then, the fourth son gave him life. As soon as the long-maned, ferocious-eyed, sharp-toothed lion came alive, he killed all four of them and ate them.

'King, what do you think about these brothers?' the vetala asked Vikramaditya. 'Who among them was the biggest fool?'

'The one who gave the lion life,' replied Vikramaditya. 'Knowledge without common sense is of no use. Intelligence of the mind is better than book-learning. Those arrogant fools who flaunt mere book-knowledge and think they know it all are eaten alive like these foolish brothers.'

The vetala laughed in ghoulish merriment, and the corpse flew back to the shisham tree. Raja Vikramaditya also turned around and retraced his steps.

Tale Twenty-two

Which Brother's Sense Perception Is Most Acute?

'Listen to this next story, O Raja,' the vetala on Vikramaditya's shoulder said. 'You seem to be a man of discriminatory tastes. I think this tale will greatly entertain you.'

There is a city called Dharmapura that was once ruled by Raja Dharmaja. In that city was an erudite Vedic brahmin named Govinda, who was a strict adherent of dharma and well versed in all the shastras. He had four sons, Haridatta, Somadatta, Yagyadatta, and Brahmadatta—all highly educated and brilliant. They were also obedient sons and diligently completed whatever tasks their father assigned.

As fate would have it, Govinda's eldest son, Haridatta, suddenly died. Govinda was so devastated that he stopped engaging in all his regular activities such as teaching, advising, and discoursing. Hearing about Govinda's grief, the king's priest, Vishnusharma, came to console him. 'Suffering is the fate of a human being, Govinda,' he said. 'It starts from the moment he's conceived in the mother's womb. When he's born, he comes into the world crying. Then, as a youth, controlled by lust and desires, he suffers jealousy and heartache. As he grows older, his body turns traitorous and slowly, he succumbs to its diseases. So, you see, pain and grief are a constant in a human being's life, like the Great Time. It has a smattering of happiness, but, overall, its essence is sorrow. No one can escape this fact.

'Even if you were to climb to the very top of the tallest tree, or sit on the highest peak of the highest mountain, or hide in the deepest water, or take up residence in a closed iron cage, or escape to patala, sorrow will find you. No matter who you are—pandit, fool; rich, poor; learned, uneducated; powerful, weak—no one is spared the onslaught of Kala. A man's life is about a hundred years; fifty are wasted in sleep. Out of the remaining, one half is spent in childhood and old age, and the other half in partings, bereavement, mourning, and sorrow. To add to that, the heart is capricious, like the waves of water. How can it guarantee any happiness?

'Besides this, O Govinda, Kaliyuga extorts its own price. In this era of darkness, truthful men are hard to find. Dharma, austerity, truth—all good values decrease every day. Kingdoms are destroyed and kings are led by greed. The earth yields less and less, while evil men, feeling entitled, snatch and grab everything. Rulers are crooked, brahmins are greedy, men become henpecked, and women become capricious. Also, sons criticize fathers, and friends become enemies. This Great Time is so immutable that it didn't even spare Abhimanyu, whose father was Arjuna and whose uncle was Krishna himself; he was killed when he was a mere youth. Creatures on earth, creatures flying in the sky, and creatures living in the water—everyone is cut down by Kala. And look at the irony of it: Lakshmi may be residing with you, your home may be filled with relatives—mother, father, wife, son, brother, and other kin—but when Yama's messenger comes to take you, no one can stop him. In fact, these very people who are connected to your life take you to the cremation ground and burn you.

'Just as the night passes and the day dawns, just as the moon sets and the sun rises, in the same way, youth ebbs and old age arrives. And time passes. Look at the blindness of man—despite seeing it all, he remains ignorant and mourns his sorrows. In this world, who is free of sorrow? Even great warriors like Yudhishthira had to bow before Inexorable Time. No amount of wealth or money can save you or accompany you to the other world. The only thing that goes with you is your own karma—your goodness, your evilness, your sins, and your good actions. Dear Govinda, I tell you, it's a waste of time to cry and wail; instead, perform acts of dharma.'

Vishnusharma's words comforted Govinda and taking the priest's advice, he decided to spend the rest of his life in dharma and asceticism. With this intention, he told his remaining three sons that he would like to perform a large yajna, a fire sacrifice, and for its success, he needed the presence of Vishnu. 'Go to the sea,' he said to them, 'and get me a tortoise, who is Vishnu in his Kurma avatar.'

The brothers set off towards the sea but instead of catching a tortoise themselves, they hired a fisherman for one hundred and one coins and had him cast his net. When the fisherman brought them the tortoise, the second eldest, Somadatta, said to Yagyadatta, the middle brother, 'You hold it.' Yagyadatta turned to the youngest, Brahmadatta, and said to him, 'Can you hold it?'

'I can't,' said Brahmadatta. 'If I touch it, my hands will stink. Then, when I touch my food, the food will also stink. You know I'm particular about my food.'

'I can't touch that slimy thing either,' said Yagyadatta. 'You know how particular I am about my women. How can I touch a woman with slimy hands?'

'And I'm particular about the bed I sleep on,' said Somadatta, the eldest. 'That's why I can't touch that tortoise, or I'll get its smell and slime all over my bed.'

In this way, the three brothers began to quarrel about who would carry the tortoise to bring to their father. Finally, they decided to leave it with the fisherman and go to the king to resolve their dispute and determine who should carry the tortoise. In the king's court, they explained their situation, and then each one stated his concern: 'I'm particular about my food,' said the youngest. 'I'm particular about my women,' said the middle brother. 'I'm particular about the bed I sleep in,' said the second-eldest.

'Let's put each of your claims to the test, starting with the youngest,' the king said and ordered his kitchen to prepare all kinds of savoury dishes. 'Eat to your heart's content,' he said to Brahmadatta.

After the feast, when Brahmadatta returned to court, the king asked him, 'Did you enjoy the food?'

'I couldn't eat a thing, Maharaj,' Brahmadatta replied.

'Why is that?'

'It was stinking.'

'What was it stinking of?'

'Maharaj, the rice was from a field located near a cremation ground. It smelt of dead bodies and I couldn't eat a morsel of it.'

The king sent his men to make an enquiry and sure enough, they reported that the rice was, indeed, from a field adjacent to the cremation ground.

Next, the king tested Yagyadatta, the middle brother. He sent him to a comfortable room that was neither warm nor cold, but just right. It was fragrant with lotuses and the bed was made with silken sheets. Sitting on the bed was a beautiful woman with her head lowered in modesty. Smiling, Yagyadatta came to sit beside her and engaged her in flirtatious banter. Then, shifting closer to her, he took her in his arms and lay down. However, as soon as he came face to face with her, he turned and faced the other way, and that is how he spent the whole night.

The following morning, when the king summoned Yagyadatta and asked him if he had had a satisfying night, he replied, 'Not at all, Maharaj. The woman you sent me—her mouth smelt like a goat.'

The king then called the bawd who had brought the young woman from her brothel and asked her who she was.

'She's my niece,' the bawd replied. 'My sister died when the girl was three months old. I'm the one who brought her up.'

'How did you feed her when she was a child?' the king asked.

'I had a goat and I fed her goat's milk during her childhood.'

Finally, the king prepared to test Somadatta. He ordered that the most comfortable bed in the palace be put in his room. It was made with many layers of mattresses and topped with sheets of thick silk. The idea of sleeping in such a luxurious bed appealed to Somadatta and he lay down in it with a deep sigh. However, after only a few moments, he began to shift around and spent the rest of the night tossing and turning. In the morning, when he was summoned to court and asked how he slept, he replied, 'Maharaj, I didn't sleep a wink.'

'Why is that?' the king asked.

'In the seventh layer of the mattresses is a hair. It pricked me all night.'

The king sent his men to check and sure enough, they found a small hair on the seventh mattress.

'Now, tell me, O Raja, which brother do you think was the most sensitive?' the vetala asked Vikramaditya.

'The brother who was particular about the bed he slept in,' Vikramaditya replied.

'How did you come to that conclusion?'

'The other two brothers had a direct sensory encounter. The one who was particular about food actually smelt the rice. The one who was particular about women came face to face with the woman and smelt her breath. But the one who was particular about his bed didn't so much as see the hair or even touch it, yet he felt it.

The vetala acknowledged Vikramaditya's response by flying the dead body back to the shisham tree.

Tale Twenty-three

Why Did the Old Brahmin Cry and Then Laugh While Switching Bodies?

As before, Raja Vikramaditya cut the corpse loose and threw it over his shoulder. Just as he began to walk towards the bargad tree, the vetala said again, 'O Raja, you are toiling so hard. Let me tell you another story to alleviate your stress.'

The city of Vishvapura was once ruled by king Vidagdha. In that city was a brahmin named Narayana, who had spent his entire life learning and mastering various arts. Among these was the art of transporting himself into another body. However, Narayana was old and decrepit, and he often said to himself, 'I want to do so much more in this life, but this old body is such a hindrance. I wish I had a young and healthy body.'

In Vishvapura was an ashram that Raja Vidagdha had constructed for brahmins to live comfortably with their families. In that ashram, a brahmin called Yagyasena had made a home for himself and his wife and young son. The boy was obedient and well behaved, and because he had been exposed to scholarly men of learning from a very early age, he knew all the shastras before he turned sixteen. Needless to say, he was the apple of his parents' eye and Yagyasena was very proud of him.

However, as it was fated, the boy became gravely sick from a fever that couldn't be cured, and he passed away. His devastated parents completed his last rites and then, accompanied by their relatives and brahmins from the ashram, they carried his corpse to the cremation ground. As his body was placed on the pyre, everyone started wailing again, lamenting the loss of such a young life.

The old brahmin, Narayana, lived near the cremation ground. When he heard the loud outcry, he stepped out of his hut, curious to see whose passing was being lamented with such fervour. When he discovered that the body on the pyre was that of a young, sixteen-year-old boy, he burst into tears. But then he laughed out loud, and, abandoning his own old body, he entered the young body on the pyre.

When people saw the boy on the pyre come alive, they were amazed. 'It's a miracle!' they exclaimed, and the ecstatic parents of the sixteen-year-old rushed to help their son off the pyre. 'How did this happen?' they asked, embracing him.

'Lord Shiva has granted me re-life,' the boy replied. 'But with the condition that in my new life I must pursue only knowledge. A true yogi is he who dries up the river of hope with asceticism, who stills his senses and concentrates only on his mind. Desire never ends; one's body may wither, teeth may fall out, legs may not stand without the aid of a walking stick, but desire remains acute. This is how life passes—day, night, week, month, and year, childhood, old age; it goes on. Human beings are born, and then they die; all who are born must die. Each one has his own desires and his own way to fulfil those desires. This life is like a dream; sometimes it's a happy dream, and sometimes, it becomes sad. But the wise know how to avoid the pitfalls of hope and desire; they shun anger and lust, and dressed only in one garment, head shaved, walking barefoot, they spend their life in pilgrimage. Therefore, dear parents and relatives, I must leave you and go on a pilgrimage.'

'This is how the old man began to live in a teenager's young body,' said the vetala to Vikramaditya. 'The question I have for you is this: why did this old brahmin cry and then laugh before entering the boy's body? And let me warn you again that if you know the answer and don't tell me, your head will shatter into a thousand pieces.'

'I know the answer,' Vikramaditya replied. 'He cried because he had spent all his life in his body and was sad to separate from it. And he laughed because the prospect of living in a young body made him happy.'

As soon as Vikramaditya gave the answer, the corpse on his shoulder shot off and hung itself on a branch of the shisham tree.

Tale Twenty-four

What Is This Riddle of Relationships?

The blackness of night was like a dark-complexioned rakshasi, and the embers of the dying pyres were like her eyes. Unfazed by this nightmarish environment, Raja Vikramaditya patiently climbed the shisham tree again, cut the corpse loose, and jumped down. As he lifted the dead body on his shoulder and turned to walk in the direction of the bargad tree, the vetala said to him, 'O Raja, I'm quite bored of this game. But I'm impressed that you are neither bored, nor have you lost interest in completing this task. So, let's try another story. This one is sure to confuse you. Listen!'

In a city lived a king by the name of Mandalika, whose wife Chandravati was the daughter of the king of Malwa. The two also had a daughter, whom they had named Lavanyavati. At about the time when the daughter came of age, Raja Mandalika's relatives cheated him out of his kingdom and all his wealth. Afraid for the safety of his family, the raja fled to Malwa with his wife and daughter, carrying with him as many jewels as he could. The first night that they were fleeing, they found themselves in Vindhya Forest, a territory that was infested by Bhils, who were known for their plundering and robbing. As they neared a Bhil village, Mandalika told his wife and daughter to hide. 'We may encounter Bhil robbers, and if I have to worry about your safety, I'll not be able to fight them,' he said. Hence, the queen and the princess found a thick grove and carefully concealed themselves. They were just in time, because right at that moment, a band of Bhils came out of the trees and fell upon the king with swords and knives. Mandalika fought valiantly, but ultimately, the chief of the Bhils killed him, and the others stole all the jewels he was carrying.

The queen and the princess were devastated at the raja's death. They were also terrified that the murderous robbers would find them and kill them as well. To escape them, they crept out of their hiding spot and went deeper into the forest. As they trudged and slogged, utterly exhausted, they came upon a lotus lake beside an ashoka tree and decided to rest. After washing themselves, they sat down under the tree with a sigh of relief. However, sitting there, holding onto each other, the realization hit them that they were alone and helpless, and this made them weep.

At that time, a local chieftain, Chandasimha, and his son, Simhaparkarma, were hunting in the forest. When they saw two sets of footprints leading from the trees to the lake, they wondered to whom they belonged. The footprints appeared to be of women; one set of feet was larger than the other. 'Let's follow these footprints,' Chandasimha said to his son. 'If we find these women, you can choose one of them and make her your wife.'

'I'd like to marry the lady who has the smaller feet, because she's obviously younger and will suit my age. But you, too, need a wife, Father. You must marry the older one with the bigger feet.'

'Son, your mother passed away only recently. She was a virtuous woman and the best wife a man could have. I have no wish to marry again.'

'Father, a householder's home is not complete without a

wife. You know what they say—a house without a wife is like a prison without chains. Besides, if you don't marry, I won't marry either.'

'Don't say that, Son,' Chandasimha said. 'Fine. If you promise to get married to the woman with the smaller feet, I, too, shall consider taking the woman with the larger feet as wife.'

Then, following the footprints, the men found the women, who were sitting beside the lotus lake, crying. Queen Chandravati was a dark beauty, and with the shining pearls around her neck, she looked as brilliant as the night sky. And Princess Lavanyavati was fair and glowing, like moonlight emanating from a full moon.

When the women saw the two men on horses, they became fearful, thinking they were robbers, but Chandasimha quickly allayed their fears. 'Don't be afraid,' he said. 'I'm a chieftain of Vittpapuri, and this is my son. We were hunting in this forest and saw your footprints. Please tell us why you're crying. Also, tell us what two beautiful, high-born women are doing in this forest all alone and unprotected.'

Wiping her tears, Chandravati told the men the sad story about why they were fleeing to Malwa, and how her husband had lost his life fighting with the Bhils.

'We're at your service,' Chandasimha said. 'My son and I propose marriage to you and to your daughter.'

The two women accepted the proposals and went with the chieftain and his son to Vittpapuri, where the son married the queen, because she had the smaller feet, and the father married the daughter, whose feet were bigger. Thus, the daughter became her mother's mother-in-law, and the mother became her daughter's daughter-in-law. They lived happily with their husbands in Vittpapuri and had many children.

After the vetala finished telling this story, he said to Vikramaditya, 'O Raja, are you ready for my question? If you know the answer to it, you must speak it.'

'What's the question?' Vikramaditya asked.

'What was the relationship of the children that were born to the mother and the daughter who were married to the son and the father?'

Vikramaditya tried to figure out the relationship of the children born from these marriages, but it was like a riddle, and he didn't know the answer to it. Hence, he remained quiet. But he continued to walk towards the bargad.

'Do you have an answer?' the vetala asked. 'Let me remind you that if you know it and don't give it, your head will shatter into a thousand pieces.'

Vikramaditya kept walking in silence, intent on delivering the corpse to Kshantisheela.

The vetala on his shoulder laughed gleefully. 'O Raja, you have answered all the questions so far, but it seems that you don't know the answer to this one. Yet, you're not afraid. You walk on with steady steps, completing the task that the tantric yogi has given you, even though the night is dark, your mission is ghoulish, and the threat of your head shattering into a thousand pieces looms over you. Your fearlessness is truly remarkable. That's why I want to give you some advice that will save your life. The ascetic, Kshantisheela, who has sent you to bring this corpse to him, is actually waiting for you to bring me to him as well. This corpse is just a means to summon me so that he can control me. And he also has a plan for you. As soon as he receives this dead body, he'll kill you. You see, to complete his sadhana to gain control over me, he needs to make a sacrifice, and you're it. Once he has sacrificed you, he'll be able to use me to acquire mastery in the magic of the vidyadharas. Then, he can enjoy all the pleasures of the earth. If you want to live, you must destroy him—without hesitation. This is my advice: if someone does you harm, you must do him harm; evil must be dealt with by any means possible. Listen to me carefully and do as I say. When Kshantisheela tells you to prostrate yourself on the ground with all eight limbs touching the earth, ask him to demonstrate how, and when he lies down to show you, cut off his head. Kill him before he kills you. Then the mastery he's hoping to gain will be yours, and you'll become the master, and all the pleasures will be yours to enjoy as well. That will be my reward to you. Now, O Raja, I'm leaving this body. Take it to the tantric yogi and do as I've instructed.'

With an unearthly laugh that echoed in every corner of the cremation ground, the vetala left the corpse.

How the Story Ends

As soon as the vetala left the dead body, Raja Vikramaditya felt the air around him change. It became more alive with the sounds of death—the sizzling of dripping flesh and the sudden sparking in smouldering fires; the crackling of scorched bones as they tumbled from pyres; the wailing of bhutas and pretas as they flitted around aimlessly, clinging to remnants of earthly existence; the screeching of night birds as they shot from tree to tree; and the constant weeping of grievers that never seemed to fade. Firmly holding the corpse on his shoulder, Vikramaditya walked decisively toward the bargad tree, under which Kshantisheela was waiting for him. When he reached it, he lifted the body and laid it on the ground before the tantric yogi, who was sitting cross-legged and chanting mantras with great intensity. 'I've done what you asked me to do, Yogi,' Vikramaditya said. 'Here's the dead body that was hanging in the shisham tree.'

'You are indeed a brave man,' Kshantisheela said, getting up. 'Your legend is not false. I'm grateful to you for helping me.' Then, taking a water pot, he poured water into the cup of his hand and uttering a mantra, sprinkled it on the corpse. After that, squatting on the ground, he drew a large mandala and placed the body in it, turning its face towards the south. He then offered worship with betel nuts, flowers, incense, and a diya, and once that was concluded, he said to Vikramaditya, 'O Raja, I want to thank you for completing the difficult task I gave you. To reward you, I want to help you gain a siddhi by which you can fulfil all your desires. Lie down on the ground and prostrate yourself with all your eight limbs touching the earth.'

'I'm a king, O Yogi,' Vikramaditya replied, 'I've never prostrated myself. I don't know how to. But if you show me, I'll learn.'

Kshantisheela lay down on the ground in prostration with his limbs and torso touching the earth. As soon as he lowered his head, Vikramaditya pulled out his khanda and sliced his neck, severing his head from his body. Then, using the tantric's skull bowl, he collected the blood that was streaming from the headless body and offered it to the vetala.

Instantly, the vetala became present. 'O great King, I congratulate you. You now have the power of eight siddhis. You can become as minute as an atom, as big as a mountain, as light as air, and as heavy as rock. You can make yourself invisible, and you have control over the will of others. You can fulfil all your desires, and you will be the lord of the world.'

As soon as the vetala made this pronouncement, a host of vidyadharas descended from the sky. Showering flowers on Vikramaditya, they hailed him as the greatest and bravest of all men and gave him sovereignty over all vidyadharas. Then, Indra, along with Brahma, Vishnu, and Mahesha, and a host of gods appeared in the sky in their flying chariots and praised Vikramaditya, calling his actions rightful. 'We are very pleased with what you have accomplished today. Ask for a boon,' they said.

'The only boon I want is that this story of twenty-four tales of vetala should become renowned in the world,' Vikramaditya said.

'It is granted,' they declared. 'As long as the moon, sun, and earth remain fixed in their places, you, your reign, and your story, along with these tales of vetala, will be celebrated in the world.'

Then Shiva hailed him as a jewel among monarchs

and announced, 'You are my essence, a portion of me—Vikramaditya, Sun of Valour. You will have dominion over the world.'

After the gods and the vidyadharas returned to their abodes, Vikramaditya, too, came back to his palace. In time, he conquered the whole world and became a Chakravarti Raja, and his glory shone brighter than the sun.

Here ends *Vetala Panchavimshati.*

Acknowledgements

Aienla, you're my team, and I'm lucky to have you. Thank you for being such a phenomenal editor.

Pinaka De, thank you for the stunning cover illustration. It has added a wow factor to this book.

Bena Sareen, a big thank you for yet another arresting cover design.

Babu, your excitement for my books is always motivating. But your eagerness to read my retelling of your favorite childhood classic has made this project very special for me.